# ALASKAN
# FAMILY
# TIES

LILY J. HANN

eBook ASIN: B0FSYBZ4CF

Paperback ISBN: 979-8-9998628-1-5

Published by: Lily Hann, Maryland, USA

Cover Design by: Madisyn Carlin, Mountain Peak Edits & Designs

Edited by: Madisyn Carlin, Mountain Peak Edits & Designs

# Contents

To my husband, for always believing in me and being my rock.

"I am with you and will watch over you wherever you go, and I will bring you back to this land. I will not leave you until I have done what I have promised you."
Genesis 28:15

# Chapter 1

Nalani Price got out of the SUV and slammed the door, still grumbling under her breath. The slam echoed off the trees around her. She could probably scream and no one, except maybe other guests, would hear her for miles. The thought filled her with a sense of peace one moment then made her heart kick into high gear. That also meant if someone killed her, no one would hear her cries for help.

Nalani shook her head. There were no serial killers in nowhere Alaska. Whoever watched her in Chicago had no idea where she was. Straightening her spine, she walked toward the cabin, her steps silent on the layer of pine needles.

"Please be unlocked." Nalani reached forward and grasped the knob. This is where her foster mother would tell her to pray, but prayer never seemed to work for her.

Others sure, but not Nalani. She was the forgotten one. Even God didn't listen to her pleas.

When the knob gave way, she lifted her brows. Her brother never left his home unlocked back in the city. Guess people change when they've been gone long enough.

"Paul, you in here?" Nalani stood in the open room.

The cabin was small, but the windows and open floor plan gave it a larger feel. She ran her fingers along the back of the recliner which sat next to the matching couch. Opposite of them was a TV mounted above a gas fireplace. Along the far wall was a small table with three chairs.

She turned towards the back of the cabin, passing the kitchen that didn't look like anyone had recently used it. Figured. Paul was always ordering take-out back home. She shook her head. A trip to the general store and a home-cooked meal might persuade him to tell her why he was ignoring her.

"Come on, Paul." She called out, hoping the vibrato would calm her. "Don't you try to scare me. I'm not defenseless anymore. I will hit you back if startled."

The nerve endings on her arm hummed. She paused and considered going back to the car to get the Ruger she had started carrying with her. It was still locked in the lockbox in her suitcase. The hassle was worth it because she didn't want to be without since someone started watching her. The police in Chicago wouldn't help her. Not until the creep did something more aggressive.

Her phone's ringing made her jump. Nalani needed to pull herself together. She was sure no one followed her here.

Her boss's number flashed across the screen. Disappointment crashed with frustration as she resisted the urge to roll her eyes at the editor-in-chief of the Chicago Times.

"Not now." She shoved the phone back in her pocket. "You'll get your story just as soon as I find my brother."

Peering into the back bedroom where a few things lay in a row on the dresser, her hope of finding Paul here was starting to fade quickly. The queen-sized bed was perfectly made complete with military-style tucked-in corners. Something he taught her to do to help her feel more secure as she slept. He was always looking out for her.

Not finding him in the master bathroom, she walked back through the kitchen to the stairs. Overlooking the living area was a loft. Maybe he was up there listening to music and couldn't hear her calling. The iron railing felt cool and smooth as her hand glided along. The loft was as neat as the bedroom. A desk with a closed laptop was positioned to face the stairs.

*"Never put your back to a door. It allows you to be vulnerable to a tickle attack."*

Nalani hung her head. What she wouldn't give to only have to worry about a tickling match between siblings.

"Where are you, Paul?" she whispered as if disturbing the silence too much would somehow make him disappear forever.

She flopped on the winged back chair positioned in the corner closest to the sliding glass door which led to a small balcony. The round end table held a lamp and Paul's Bible. He wouldn't have left without it. Maybe he was just at work and would soon be back.

Nalani picked up the worn leather book. He clearly used his more than she did hers. A sigh escaped her lips. Flipping the pages an envelope fell into her lap. Picking the package up carefully, her brother's boxy handwriting scrolled across the front. Her name and address were written, but no postage.

It had been a long time since he chose to write her a letter. Email, text, or call were faster. Had he found something about her past that he didn't want in an electronic trail?

The last time they talked she bugged him to spill what he was doing up in Alaska. He relented after her constant barrage of inquiry. He confessed to following a lead about her mother. He refused to tell her anything until he confirmed it.

She turned the envelope over and carefully pulled out the blue paper. Unfolding the note, an SD card bounced off her leg and onto the floor.

As she bent to pick up the tech, she felt something hard press into her side.

"Give me the card," a low voice growled at her. Her brain froze for a moment.

Paul was going to send her this card. There was no way she was going to just give it over to some thug who got the drop on her. She should never have let her guard down.

Nalani visualized the room and catalogued the nearest weapon's position was in relation to where she stood. The lamp was just out of reach. The Bible lay on the chair. She needed to get distance from this guy. It looked like she'd have to do it on her own.

With slow movements, she started to turn towards her assailant.

The gun dug into her ribs. "Don't turn around, just hand me the card."

"Alright. Here." With all her strength she rammed her elbow back connecting with the man's neck.

The pressure of the gun fell away as gasping came from behind her. She didn't have time to look at her attacker. She leapt for the stairs only to have her shirt yanked, toppling her backwards.

A strong arm slid around her shoulders and the gun returned to her side. "Not so fast."

Hot breath skidded across her cheek as she fought the roil of her stomach at the rancid smell of body odor. She needed to break his hold. "Don't make me hurt a pretty little thing like you," he hissed. "Give me the card."

She needed to buy time to come up with another way out. "Why are you doing this?"

"Hand it over." He slid his arm to her neck. Her lungs burned for a full breath and dots danced on her peripheral.

She grabbed and scratched his arm. He grunted at her effort but did not wane.

"Okay." She tapped at the beefy arm. The pressure on her throat released. She gulped in blessed air.

Pushing off the floor, she swept her leg around. The man thudded to the ground. Taking the stairs two at a time, she shoved the SD card into the side pocket of her pants. Why hadn't she brought her gun into the house?

This time she made it to the first floor when a weight hit her in the back. She slammed into the wood flooring. The air rushed from her lungs.

She groaned then felt herself being flipped over. She couldn't see past the barrel pointed at her face.

"Don't move."

She swallowed. Despite their fight, the gun was solid in the man's hand. This man was a trained fighter. His other hand pressed along her abdomen where the pockets on her jacket lay.

He moved on to her front pants pockets. She had never been so happy for a pair of pants with lots of pockets as she was right now.

A low growl came from his throat. He ran his hand towards her side pockets. She was running out of time but with the gun less than an inch from her face, there wasn't much she could do.

The sound of a car outside made the man bolt back up the stairs. Nalani sat up dazed for a moment. Should she run outside towards the car? Or should she go back upstairs to get the note that she dropped?

The sliding door being opened had her moving towards the steps. Her attacker had fled. She needed to see what was on that note. If Paul was home, he could take the guy out as he was trying to escape off the balcony.

The blue paper still lay on the floor next to the chair. She picked it up.

Before she could read it, the front door opened. She'd simply ask him in person. Shoving the note into the pocket of her jacket she ran toward the stairs.

"Paul!" She bounded down the first three steps.

A cold hard voice boomed up the steps to greet her, "FBI! Stop!"

Special Agent Davin Schulz held his gun steady as he approached the intruder.

The woman's eyes widened. Her hair was skewed like she had just woken from a nap or been in a fight.

Her hands trembled in front of her, "I...I didn't break in. The door was open, and Paul said that I could come visit him any time." She tipped her chin up. "I wasn't going to come anytime soon with deadlines to meet, but when he didn't return my calls, I had to come find him. The guy who attacked me just ran out the sliding glass door. You should be pointing that thing at him." Her voice rose with each statement.

He lowered his gun slightly. She held his gaze. He wouldn't put it past Spartak, the organization he was tracking, to send someone to see what Paul found. "Who attacked you?"

"I don't know. Isn't that your job to figure out?" she ground out.

Davin stared at the woman. Her clenched jaw made her look like she would take on the world. He switched his tactic. "How do you know Paul?"

She took a deep breath, "He's my brother."

Davin had interviewed Paul himself. The man didn't have any siblings.

The muscles in his arm coiled. He widened his stance. Who was she really?

"Paul never mentioned a sister." He kept his doubts from his voice as much as he could.

She pressed her shoulders back. "Who exactly are you? How do I know you're not working with the guy who just attacked me?"

"I didn't see anyone leave when I came in," he tried to reassure her.

"I already told you. He went out the sliding glass door up here." She nodded behind her.

Davin started up the stairs. "Sit in the chair."

Keeping the woman in his view, he walked to the balcony. Scanning the area, he saw no movement. Whoever was here, was long gone now.

Davin holstered his gun and turned toward the woman. "Tell me again how you know Paul?"

She crossed her arms over her chest. "He's my foster brother. His parents were my last placement before I aged out. He's the closest thing I have to family." She let her hands fall to her lap. "Even if he never mentioned me to you."

If she was an agent for Spartak, she was a gifted actress, but his gut told him she spoke the truth.

"Do you know where he is? Is he just in town? Where else could he be?"

Her questions came rapid fire, and it took his brain a moment to catch up with the barrage. "I came here to find Van Kirk. He failed to check in two days ago."

Davin and his team had been working for months to take down the Russian mob. Paul had volunteered to go undercover to gain information about the mob's next move.

The group hadn't been active in the States for a few decades, but there was chatter that the power in the organization was shifting. They had turned their attention to Alaska and Davin needed to figure out what they had planned before anyone was killed.

"What do you mean, failed to check in? My brother was up here researching my past or at least that's what he said he was doing." She leaned closer and got within inches. Her brown eyes had flecks of gold in them that made them sparkle.

Davin took a step back. Taking down this organization needed to remain his sole focus. He couldn't be distracted by a pair of pretty eyes.

Besides, Sharron taught him that a woman didn't want to share him with his career. Which needed to be his sole focus now.

Especially when he didn't even know if she was telling the truth.

"Paul VanKirk is on my team." Davin turned away and looked around. He needed to search the whole place. "He was on assignment when we lost contact with him."

"Where did you send him? What was his assignment?" He heard her step up behind him. "Please don't tell me he's dead."

Davin swung around and raised his hands. "We don't know what happened. I can't tell you details about his assignment except that we're looking for him."

According to Paul's last report, Spartak was smuggling something through the port at Seward. What that was or where it came from were still unknown. Why the group had broken into a scientist's lab and stolen research on waterways was also a mystery. One they needed to figure out.

If the rumors were true, they didn't have long before the group graduated from smuggling to terrorism.

She breathed in through her nose and out through her mouth. Her high cheeks and tanned skin reminded him of an Inuit warrior. She was beautiful, but off limits.

"Can you please tell me your name?" He needed to learn more about her. She might have an idea where Paul would be.

"My name..." She glanced past him.

He waited her out.

"My name is Nalani. Nalani Price. I'm here looking for Paul, but we've already covered that."

She hugged her arms around her middle and stepped to the window. When she turned back tears brimmed her eyes. "Please, you have to help me find him. He's all I have."

Sunlight flickered off glass just inside the tree line. Davin's elbow glanced off the wood floor as he slammed into her. He wrapped his arms around her head and covered her with his body.

Glass rained across his back. A few shards slipped beneath his collar.

He waited for another shot. When one didn't come, he whispered into her ear. "Stay here."

There were no more shots, but that didn't mean that the shooter wasn't still out there waiting for a second chance. The question was, who were they aiming at?

Nalani....or him?

Davin rolled over and angled himself to look out the window. The shadows made it near impossible to see very far. "I can't see much. I'm going to go out the front. Stay down and hidden."

Davin crouch-ran to the front door, where he peeked through the lowest pane.

No movement.

He opened the door and took the steps with his head ducked. Stayed low and ran as quick as he could.

Davin made his way to the backside of the house. The rough bark of the cabin dug into his back, but he kept himself pressed as flat as he could. He scanned the area where he had seen the reflection and still saw no movement.

He pulled out his phone and sent a message to Taylor Ertz, the other agent assigned to his field office. She could check the woods while he secured Nalani.

As he turned to return to the front, a paper was pegged to the log of the house. Keeping his gun in his shooting hand, he removed the note from the side of the house careful to use the edge of his jacket to preserve evidence.

He needed to get back to Nalani. Entering the space, he scanned where he had left her. It was empty. The note felt like lead in his pocket, but he needed to secure her and the house first, then he would read it.

Keeping his gun at the ready, Davin made his way back the short hall towards the bedroom. A shadow crossed beneath the closed door.

"Nalani if that's you, open up. It's me, Davin."

The door flew open and Nalani stood there with a lamp in her other hand. "What took you so long?"

"I don't believe they are there anymore, but I have another agent checking it out. Until I hear otherwise, we'll need to stay put." Davin swept past her to the window next to the bed. Pulling the curtain shut he gestured for her to close the door.

"Come away from the door, but keep the lamp."

A smirk started on her face. "It's not even a knife at this gun fight."

Davin had to resist the urge to chuckle. He wasn't sure she was joking or being serious, but that hint of a smile drew his attention. She had this beauty that radiated from within.

*Stop staring. She's Paul's sister. You have a job to do.* He signaled for her to sit in the chair next to the dresser. Away from the door and any potential threat.

Placing himself between her and the rest of the cabin, he pulled a pair of gloves from the inside pocket of his jacket and carefully took the note out. He preferred wearing the FBI jacket to a suit jacket any day for the pockets alone.

"What is that?" Her voice was quiet but he could feel her close by. Turning around put him inches from her. Again. Even in the darkened room the gold in her eyes mesmerized him. He took a step backwards and angled himself away from her. *Get your head in the game, Schulz.*

"It was tacked to the back of the house." He unfolded it only to have the words make his blood run cold.

Give me what I want or the girl dies.

# Chapter 2

Nalani gasped as she stared at the scribbled words. "Is that referring to me? I just got here." She stumbled back and sunk into the chair.

How had she gone from a possible stalker in Chicago to the target of an Alaskan bad guy?

She got up and started to pace the small space. "What exactly are you supposed to be giving back? What have you gotten my brother into?"

She had worried about Paul ever since he went to Quantico. To think she could be the reason he was dead and not his job.

Davin winced before his indifferent mask fell back into place. His hard jaw and short-cropped hair screamed FBI agent. He took his career seriously. That much was obvious. She should probably cut him some slack.

"I can't tell you specifics. You're just going to have to trust me when I say that Paul knows what he's doing and I'm going to do everything in my power to find him."

Davin's phone rang. Nalani jumped.

"Schulz."

She watched Special Agent Davin Schulz pace the small space. It wasn't lost on her that she was essentially locked in her brother's bedroom with a handsome man.

"Thank you, Ertz." He turned back to her. "The area has been cleared. I'm going to need to take your official statement."

"This time without the gun pointed at me would be nice." She lifted her chin towards the gun still in his hand.

Davin holstered his gun and followed her out to the living room. She flopped onto the couch, staring at the broken window.

He cleared his throat. "Let's start at the beginning."

She should probably tone down her tendency toward sarcasm before she made the serious FBI agent man even more agitated.

He had seemed sincere when he was protecting her just now. The way he had put himself between her and the entry point of the room had given her a feeling of safety she was unaccustomed to-but which reassured her more than she wanted to admit.

The dark and brooding type hadn't ever been her thing. When he had been so close there for a moment though, the concern deep in those silver-blue eyes had her reconsidering her no-more-dating rule. No guy ever stuck around. It was easier never to date than give her heart cause to hope.

"Like I said before. I came to find Paul." Nalani brushed back hair from her cheek. "Last time we talked, he said he found something about my birth mother."

Davin shifted. She could tell he wanted to ask about that, but he waited for her to continue.

"I don't know much about my birth parents despite researching since I was 18. I even tried one of those DNA database things with no hits."

His face remained stoic. Usually people either became curious or gave her pity. Not Mr. FBI. She would have settled for a "that's too bad", but no.

"When Paul didn't return any of my calls, texts, and emails, I decided to come and find him."

She couldn't bring herself to say it, but the possibility was that Paul could be dead. All because of her.

If he found something about her mother and that got him killed, she'd never be able to forgive herself. God wouldn't be that cruel as to take the only person in her life that knew her. That continued to show up. Would He?

"We don't know what happened to Paul." Davin ran his hand through his hair. "His disappearance could just as easily be because of his work."

She bit her nail, a habit she was never able to break. "But what about the note you found outside?"

"It's a generic threat. The girl could be Agent Ertz or some other person in Paul's life." He paused briefly as if sorting out the options. "We don't even know if it was meant for me, or for Paul."

"But the girl could just as easily be me." Whoever this guy was, she'd fight for the only family she had.

"Hey." Davin rested his hand on her shoulder, sending warmth across her. "We will find him."

She instinctively pulled away and he dropped his hand. This man might be an FBI agent, but that didn't mean he wouldn't cut her loose the first chance he got. She didn't know anything about him.

All she knew was Paul was missing.

"Can you tell me what happened before we met? Did you see anything out of place?"

She closed her eyes and recounted from the moment she arrived at the lodging estate until his arrival scared the guy away.

The SD card and letter were still in her pocket. Should she tell Agent Schulz about it? It was addressed to her, but he was also looking for Paul. He also had way more resources to find her brother before it was too late. She needed to keep holding on to the hope that he was still alive.

"When I picked up his Bible, this fell out." She pulled the envelope and SD card from her pocket and handed it to him.

"Let's take a look at what Paul was going to send you. Shall we?"

She held her hand up.

"Fine," he huffed. "But I want to be with you. When you view it," he added quickly.

Nalani pressed her lips together to keep from smiling.

"Let me grab my computer unless you know Paul's password."

He shook his head and she bound out the front door before he could object. Never mind the danger of just stepping outside. The journalist in her smelled a story that needed investigating, and the sister wanted her brother back.

*Find Paul and then maybe you'll have answers to your past.* She gave herself a pep talk as she grabbed her things from the backseat.

The knowledge that Paul was "chasing after dangerous people" piqued the interest of the journalist inside her.

What dangerous people could be here in Alaska? That would be a question she would have to ask just the right way in order to get an actual answer from this FBI agent. So far he hadn't told her anything about what he and Paul had been investigating, or what might have happened to her brother.

When she turned around, he stood on the top step. Watching not just her, but their surroundings. She ran past him into the house. The scowl on his face was a reminder that there was a possible threat against her.

She set her laptop on the kitchen counter and inserted the SD card.

There was only one file on the whole card. A picture of a woman in about her late 50's or early 60's appeared on the screen. She had straight dark hair and dark eyes that looked like they held many secrets.

"Who are you?" Nalani whispered.

"I don't know."

She spun around, touching a hand to her front. "Davin." She didn't know he'd come near.

"Didn't mean to scare you. Is this the only thing on here?" He pointed to the screen.

Davin moved closer which meant that their shoulders were almost touching. His spicy aftershave wafted over her. Why did he have to smell good too? He looked at her expectantly and she realized he'd asked a question.

Nalani nodded. "I'm going to do an image search to see if I can find her online. Just as soon as I can find enough signal for a connection." She pulled out her phone. Only about half bars. Not going to be the fastest search, but it would have to do.

Davin held up his phone. He had the WiFi screen pulled up showing the password for the cabin. "It's not a secure network, but I figured for what we need to use it for, we'll be fine."

"Good to know. I'll turn on my VPN before searching." The search engine populated results only a moment after she got signed on. "That was faster than I thought."

"There." He pointed to the exact picture that Paul left on the card. "Kaya Fisher, Director of Chugachmiut."

"What's Chugachmiut?" She slowed down the strange word to pronounce it correctly.

"It's a non-profit organization representing and preserving the native peoples of the Kenai Peninsula."

"Does that have to do with your case?"

Davin shrugged. "They create events that teach others about the ways of their ancestors."

"So this is about me? One of my parents was somehow connected to this organization?"

"I highly doubt this picture has anything to do with who Paul was tracking for us."

But he had no intention of telling her anything about his case? Nalani bit back the frustration. "So the Chugachmiut aren't dangerous people plotting to take over the world?"

She knew that she was being ridiculous, but it was her defense mechanism to get sarcastic. She doubted it would ruffle Mr. FBI's feathers.

He folded his arms. "They aren't dangerous."

"At least I can guess he probably didn't go missing because of me." Maybe it was bad to let hope infuse her, but she couldn't help herself. She was better off finding answers to her questions and figuring out the truth rather than succumb to the temptation of believing in a good outcome.

Especially when the worst might very well happen.

"There's only one way to find out." His expression softened a little, and she might've even seen worry under the surface. Finally he said, "Look, the only way to know for sure is to go ask her some questions."

Nalani closed her laptop. "Great. So you'll come with me?"

She winced internally as soon as she asked the question. She wasn't sure why she invited him to come along when it had been his suggestion. Even with Paul, she had always done things on her own.

Now wasn't the time to start relying on anyone. Especially a man.

Davin turned away so she couldn't get a read on his expression. "Let me just grab Paul's computer. I'll have Ertz come in and install cameras so that we'll know if someone comes back."

Nalani stilled. "You think whoever attacked me and shot at us will try again?"

Davin bent to unplug Paul's computer. "Clearly this guy thinks the SD card is somehow a danger to him."

What had Paul gotten into? Were they here to kill him?

They believed he was alive, then it meant they hadn't killed him.

They had likely wanted to search his place for something he took from them. There had to be something she was missing.

So many other questions filled her mind. She needed to pry more out of the grumpy agent in order to figure this whole thing out.

Once he was back down the stairs, she turned to leave. He put his arm out to stop her. "Let me go first this time. Just to be safe."

Davin stepped through the door with one hand on his weapon, scanning the woods for any threat. "All right. Stay close."

Nalani swiped up her computer and purse that was still on the floor. Why did this man insist on being close to her? It was making her heart want something that she knew wouldn't last.

She felt as if the shadows were staring at her. Nalani walked briskly as she could to her rental.

"We should go together in my…"

"I'm not leaving my rental here for some person to shoot at." She didn't trust a lot of people, and being without the means to leave of her own volition didn't sit right.

Davin nodded. "Good point."

She reached for her door and he opened it for her. Nalani blinked at him.

He said, "I'll lead the way, you follow."

She slid in, wondering if she could find her brother-or answers-before this man blew through her walls. She would leave, go back to Chicago, and return to her life.

Which meant she could absolutely not fall for this man.

No matter what happened.

Davin checked his rearview mirror once again. Nalani Price didn't seem like the following type. She had grit and intelligence behind that pretty face.

Two things that made his heart want things he simply couldn't have. He needed to keep his focus on terrorists threatening his country. Not to mention one of his team was missing.

"Get your head together Schulz." He spoke the admonishment out loud. Maybe this time he'd take his own advice. He had a deadly organization to take down; he didn't need to be distracted by a spitfire with silky black hair that smelled like coconut.

What he needed to do was focus on the case.

When he looked briefly through Paul's office, he hadn't seen anything that would be of help. He'd have to take the computer back with him to the office to have Ertz take a look. It felt like they were betraying his friend's privacy, but if it saved Paul's life, he'd ask for forgiveness later.

Paul's message to the team three days ago was that he was checking on a lead about bread. It didn't make any more sense now than it had then, but he knew his agent was solid. Which was why he was worried when Paul missed his check in by twenty-four hours.

If he lost an agent...

Davin had worked hard to prove himself the man for this field office since he was assigned three years ago.

He only had two other agents under him, but failure here would derail his career trajectory and they might even send him back to DC if he didn't fix this.

Just the thought of that made him shiver. He and politics didn't exactly see eye to eye, especially since his father was a US Senator. Being in the same town wasn't going to help them agree about the way things should work.

Besides, he would take a possible bear attack any day over all of that DC traffic.

His phone rang in the cupholder so he pressed the button on his car's screen to connect. "Schulz."

"Hey, Boss. I got the cameras set up and streaming to the office. You should be able to access them via the link I sent you."

"Thank you, Ertz. Finish gathering evidence from the shooting and get anything that needs a lab off to Anchorage. We are chasing down a lead. Not sure it has to do with either the shooting or Paul's disappearance, but it's worth checking out."

"We, sir?" Taylor's voice held no disrespect but peaked with curiosity.

"Paul's sister was the one in the cabin with me when the shooting started. She found a SD card that Paul was going to send to her."

Taylor didn't say anything for a second. "I didn't even know Paul had a sister."

"I didn't either." He blew out a breath. He wanted to trust her, but this was his team. "Get me what you can on Nalani Price. Just in case she isn't who she says she is."

"You got it, Boss."

Davin understood the hesitation. If Nalani was indeed Paul's sister, running a background check on her would be an invasion of privacy – at least as far as she was concerned. For him, it was a way to work toward resolving this.

If she was an employee with Spartak, they needed to know.

The call disconnected and Davin slowed to make the turn just outside of town. The Chugachmiut center was a log structure designed like a long meeting house that the Inuit people used.

Davin had nothing but respect for the native peoples of Alaska. He had the privilege of working with the elders of the tribes his first year at the Seward Field Office. Together they stopped a group of con-artists stealing people's land rights.

The elders knew the secrets of the land and understood the balance that was needed in order to keep this area of the world beautiful.

Nalani pulled her SUV in beside his. He was having a hard time getting a read on her. One moment she was opening up and telling him about her connection with Paul and then the next she was closing ranks. It was as if she wanted connection but was afraid to embrace it.

He shook his head and climbed out. Taylor had him reading too many romance novels for the office book club. He would have to suggest a thriller for the next book of the month.

He climbed out of his car and heard her say, "Look at this place. The workmanship on this building is astounding."

Davin tilted his head to study her. Not what he was expecting her to notice. She was already walking over to meet the woman who had come out of the main doors.

Kaya Fisher stood at the door with a pleasant smile on her face. "I should take you to see the gift shop. There is a local woodworker who makes intricately designed puzzle boxes, instruments, and even furniture."

Davin strode over.

Nalani said, "That sounds lovely—"

He cut her off. "But we came here to talk with you."

Kaya looked over each of them. "Looks serious." She signaled for them to follow her.

Davin held the door so Nalani could go first. He took one last scan of the surrounding area before going inside the meeting place.

Although the outside was made to represent a traditional meeting house, the inside reminded Davin more of a modern museum. Displays of artifacts showcased how the Qutekcak lived before the Russians pushed them out of their port home.

Kaya led them to an office at the back of the center. "Please have a seat."

She sat in a high-backed chair and pointed to two chairs across from a small wooden desk with scenes of bears hunting salmon and even a wolf howling. The desk must have been made by that wood carver she had mentioned.

Davin sat forward in his chair. "Thank you for talking with us, Ms. Fisher."

He caught Nalani's glare, but he wasn't going to apologize. After all, his agent was missing and he needed answers.

"Kaya is fine." She waved a hand, either not catching Nalani's icy stare or choosing to ignore it. "What can I help you with?"

"I'm Agent Schulz from the FBI and this is Nalani Price. We're looking for her missing brother who also happens to be one of my agents."

Compassion crinkled in the lines of her tanned face. She wore her hair in a long braid draped over her shoulder. The silver strands wove through the dark cord. Her presence commanded respect yet she extended gentleness to them now. "I'm so sorry your brother is missing, Nalani. How can I help you?"

Nalani sat forward on the chair. "He said that he was researching my past. I was in foster care my whole life so I don't know anything about who my parents were."

"I'm sorry, child. In the Qutekcak language, Sugt'stun we have a word for kin. *Ilat* means family. We believe in learning from our elders and passing our traditions down to our children. If I can help you find your family, I will."

Nalani pulled out her phone. "This is my brother, Paul."

Kaya's eyes widened in recognition. "I remember him. He came to speak with me last week about an accident that happened twenty-five years ago. It was sad, really. A brother and sister were traveling home when their car slid off the ice and into the bay. They froze to death before the rescue workers could get them out of the water. I remember it because my father was one of the rescue workers. He said there was nothing they could have done to save them, but I could see that it tore him up inside."

"Do you remember their names?" Nalani asked in a small voice.

"Of course." Kaya nodded. "They were both a few years behind me in school, but in a small community I still knew them. Wyatt and Lorelai Howard. Their parents were devastated, as the whole community. Such a tragic loss."

*So, Paul came here to ask about an accident?*

That didn't have anything to do with the case they were working. But it might be connected to Nalani—though, he couldn't see how.

Davin had to know if there was some connection to their case, or if this was purely personal for Paul. "Did Paul ask you about anything else?"

Kaya looked up as if seeing the conversation play back in her head. "He only asked about the Howard siblings."

Nalani shifted in her chair. "Are their parents still alive? Could I talk with them?"

"I'm afraid not." Kaya shook her head. "The only person still alive is Helen's sister. Helen was their mother."

"Where could I find her?" The hope in Nalani's voice made him want to help her find answers about who she was, but he had an agent to find and a Russian organization to shut down. Would she still be here when he was done with this case?

Or he could invite her to work alongside him?

"I could reach out to her, but she does not usually welcome visitors." Kaya pinched her mouth in a frown.

Nalani stood. "Thank you for your time then, I suppose."

Davin got up as well, digging out his wallet. "If you think of anything else about your conversation with Paul, please give me a call." He handed Kaya one of his business cards.

Davin came up beside Nalani, matching her quickened stride. "Would you like to come back to the field office with me?"

She snapped her head towards him, "You want to help me?"

He wondered why that concept seemed so surprising to her. Maybe pointing a gun at her had left a bad first impression. "We both want to find Paul. I have his computer to go through. There might be more on there to help you. If you want to look. "

"The most important thing right now is to find Paul. I've waited this long to find out about my family, I can wait a bit longer."

Davin opened the door for Nalani and scanned the area around the parking lot.

Nalani's gasp pulled his attention back to their vehicles. The passenger window on Nalani's rental had been smashed.

Davin unholstered his gun. "Get back inside. Call 911."

# Chapter 3

D avin stood guard, gazing over the parking lot and tree line until he heard the door's soft thud.

Clearing the sides of the building, he approached Nalani's vehicle. If she was working for Spartak, why would she be targeted right now? Taylor would hopefully have her background finished

He slipped his Bluetooth into his ear and hit redial.

Taylor answered after the first ring. "Seward Field Office."

"I'm bringing Nalani Price in with me." Silence met that statement. "Her car was vandalized. As soon as the police take our statements we'll be on our way. Tell me what you found about her."

"Nalani Price is a resident of Chicago where she is employed at the Tribune. She was a part of the team that won the Worth Bingham Prize for uncovering how Chicago schools were fining students for minor behaviors forcing some families into debt. She was only twenty-three at the time."

"Wow." Although her work accomplishments were impressive, he needed to know how she was connected with Paul. "What about her childhood? Were her and Paul actual foster siblings?"

"She bounced around from foster house to foster house in the Chicago area, but her last placement was with Paul's family. It was her longest one. She was there for just over eighteen months."

Davin couldn't even imagine a childhood without parents. Let alone one where a person moved so often. No wonder she didn't trust easily. That kind of upbringing would make it hard to establish connections. His own family wasn't perfect, but he knew that they were there to support him. Well at least his mother always supported his life choices. His dad was a whole different problem.

Taylor interrupted his trailing thoughts. "I've got to go. The cameras at Paul's just indicated that there was motion there. I'll check in later."

That's what Paul had said three days ago and the guy hadn't been seen since. "Keep me updated."

Davin lifted a prayer that he wouldn't lose another agent.

After giving their statements to the local police about the broken window, Nalani reported the problem with the rental company.

Nalani huffed as she put her phone back in her pocket. "They don't have another car available right now."

Davin went to his gear bag in the back. "I think I can fix it for you."

He could have suggested they leave the car, but he knew that she would want her independence even if he was fighting the urge to throw her in a safe house until they sorted this all out. Nalani was a strong woman used to being on her own. It wouldn't go over well.

Nalani followed Davin to the Seward FBI Field Office, where his team worked and sometimes lived. The office was an old storefront complete with an upper deck overlooking Fourth Avenue with a few chairs set out on it that he used sometimes to clear his head. Above the office was an apartment that they used as a locker room, break room, and a bunkhouse when necessary.

There were only three agents including himself assigned to the office. Paul was the newest and had only been there a few months.

Paul volunteered to go undercover when the chatter started about an assignation. They'd all agreed since he wasn't known to many in this part of Alaska. He had transferred from some place in Chicago, but Paul didn't say much about his time there and Davin didn't ask much beyond reading the reports involving him. Enough to know he was a solid agent even though he'd only been one for a few years.

Now he wished he would have asked more about the guy, and his personal life. Then it wouldn't have been such a surprise to find out Paul had a sister.

Davin took Paul's computer from the passenger seat and waited for Nalani at the back door. He input his code into the pad and held the door open for her, suddenly nervous about what she might think. This was nothing like her fancy Chicago newspaper.

"Welcome to Seward's Field Office."

"It looks like a cute little shop from the front, but this--" She turned, slowly sweeping her eyes over each corner. "--is impressive."

Her approval of this space expanded a bit of pride in him. She was preceptive and he found himself valuing her opinion.

The space held their three desks, a conference room with a glass wall separating it from the rest of the office space. Along the wall in the conference room was the whiteboard they used to sort out ideas.

Thankfully, Taylor had erased their brain dump from this morning involving Paul's disappearance and Spartak's next move. They knew that the group was planning an attack in Alaska, but they had yet to confirm the location or means.

Was Spartak going to set off a bomb to create mass confusion or causalities? Or were they planning a more targeted assassination? They weren't even sure who was the one pulling the strings.

When they arrested two teens for having illegal firearms in a government building, they got their first glimpse into the organization. Neither of the kids would say a word about who was a part of Spartak or what they were planning.

"The conference room would give us the most space to work." He held the door for her and she took one of the chairs with her back to the glass wall. Perfect, he would position himself at the end so that he could see out into the main office since they were the only ones here at the moment.

Davin opened Paul's personal laptop on the table. "You wouldn't happen to know his password, would you?"

"No." She wrung her hands together. "Are you sure we should be doing this? I feel like it's an invasion of Paul's privacy, but I also want to find answers. He could be in serious danger."

Davin nodded. "Those were my thoughts as well."

He tilted his head back and forth stretching the tight muscles in his neck. His computer skills weren't NSA hacker level, but he could hopefully still get into this one.

"Have you done this before?" She raised one eyebrow.

"Yes, but only in training and not to a friend's computer."

After a few minutes of trying, she sighed heavily and he sat back. Out of ideas. He felt the weight of her frustration on top on his own.

"Let me see your laptop." He extended his hand toward her.

She squinted at him. "Why?"

Again with the distrust? It would take time to earn her faith, but hopefully this olive branch would help. "I'd like to connect you to our WiFi. Then you can research about Wyatt and Lorelai, the two who died in that crash. Maybe their story can give us clues. I don't think he disappeared because of his search into them, but every lead deserves to be run to its end."

Her face relaxed a bit, but the frown still tugged at her full dark pink lips. Ones that complemented her olive complexion perfectly. "You're going to put me on your WiFi? Giving me access to your network?"

"Of course not."

Her full scowl returned.

Davin cleared his throat. "We have a network for visitors. It's standard protocol for everyone not an agent of the FBI."

"I guess that's fair." She pulled her computer out of her backpack and slid it across the table after signing in. "So you're not going to let me use APHIS to search for these two people?"

"No." He spotted a smile play at the edges of her lips. He finished connecting her to their network – with guest restrictions. "But if you need help with something, I can get Taylor to assist you when she returns."

"Where is Taylor?" She looked around the small office space.

He checked his phone. No update yet. "She's running down a lead for our case. She'll check in when she can."

He hoped. *Lord, don't let me lose another agent.*

Instead of continuing to try to manually log into Paul's computer, he opened up Taylor's hacking program on the desktop along the wall and he plugged Paul's laptop directly into it. The program would open the computer faster than he could and he had no time for his pride to get in the way of progress.

He retrieved his own computer from his desk and returned.

Nalani sat with her one leg tucked under her and her other knee pulled close to her chest. She looked so innocent and focused. It made him smile.

He tore away his gaze. *Not going to happen.* He had a Russian organization to stop and an agent to find. What was it about this woman that was messing with his concentration? The last time he allowed a pretty face to distract him, he almost got his partner killed.

He needed to try and ping Paul's phone again. It hadn't been on yesterday for them to get a current location, but the last pinged location was Paul's cabin. Opening the program he input the number.

Still not turned on.

An idea popped into his head. It was a long shot, but if it meant finding Paul before Spartak could complete their plan, than it was something he'd try.

He leaned over to Nalani. "You wouldn't happen to be able to give permission for me to access Paul's personal phone records, would you?"

"Actually, we are on the same plan."

Davin tried to keep the shock from his face.

She said, "I was working three jobs to put myself through college. Money was tight and he put me on his plan. I never left because it's more cost effective. And, well, it doesn't matter."

It didn't take FBI training to see there was more to her story. But for now, Davin chose to leave it be.

She started typing on her laptop then turned it towards him. The cell phone provider's account page had Paul's name at the top. If there was any doubt left in his mind before, it was all erased now. She really was Paul's sister. Yet another reason to make her off limits.

*All right God, thanks for this one.* They might just find him if God kept showing up like this.

Davin scrolled through the messages that Paul had received in the last week.

They were from himself, Paul's mom, Taylor, and Nalani. No secret girlfriend or other friends that he could see.

He didn't want to read the conversations he was having with his family so he clicked on the thread with Taylor. Glancing through he didn't notice anything beyond work requests or book talk. Taylor had gotten to him too – a thought that oddly comforted Davin.

He checked the call log and noticed more of the same.

The only four people Paul had any contact with were either work or family along with a few calls to Kaya Fisher which they already knew about.

There.

The day of the last ping on Paul's phone the agent got a call from an unknown number.

Davin typed the number into his laptop and it came up unregistered. It was a burner phone. He would have to try and track down where it was bought and pray that they had a picture of the person.

Davin handed the laptop back to Nalani. "Thank you. There's nothing obvious in his messages to indicate he's in danger, and I promise I didn't read the ones from you."

Nalani relaxed a bit. Had she been worried that he would discover something? Should he have read her messages? *No.* She has proven herself to be truthful, so far.

"I looked at his call log," Davin said. "Beyond work and you and his mother, the only other outgoing call in the last week was to Kaya Fisher."

Nalani's eyes narrowed. "I feel like she wasn't telling me everything. Like she told me just enough...maybe in the hope that I wouldn't ask too many questions. Maybe I should ask if she wants to meet."

He had sensed something similar about the woman they'd spoken to, but with Paul's life possibly in danger it hadn't been the time to ask about a vehicle accident. He wasn't convinced it had been Kaya just trying to get rid of him. Some people got nervous enough around cops let alone when faced with FBI agents.

He may have grown up in Anchorage, but Seward was a small town comparatively and he was still earning the trust of the people here.

"I think I'm going to go back or maybe meet her on neutral ground. I need to know if the attacks happening around me are connected to what she told Paul or not." Nalani stared up to the ceiling. "Where is the best coffee in town?"

"13 Ravens Coffee. Its down by the docks. I can take you there."

She shook her head and stood, pulling out her phone. "No, I think I'll go alone. Let me call her and see if she could meet me there."

Davin watched as she paced the space talking with Kaya. He checked his phone for an update from Taylor. Still nothing.

He didn't like Nalani going on her own. She had been threatened, shot at, and had her car window broken.

Even if her past wasn't connected to Paul's disappearance, Spartak would not hesitate to kill an innocent if it meant their plan went off. His gut tightened.

Nalani shoved her phone back into her pocket.

Davin took a step towards her to block her retreat to the door. "You shouldn't go alone. There is clearly a threat against you."

Nalani rested her hand on his upper arm. "I've been on my own my entire life. I will be fine." Then she winked and walked away.

All of the arguments to keep her close, to keep her safe, died on his lips. He wouldn't manipulate her to stay with him. He was not his father.

Nalani smiled to herself as she parked along the street in front of the old train dinning car that was turned into a café and bookstore. The look on Agent Schulz's face when she winked at him and squeezed his toned arm still made her heart tick up a few notches.

The man was intense. Good for hunting down missing agents and whatever bad guy they were all chasing.

She knew under the gruff exterior that he cared for his agents. And if she dreamed just a bit, she saw that same care flash in his eyes while he tried to get her to stay.

But he still let her go. Like he knew her drive to find the truth was important to her. That he even respected her.

She closed the door to her car and inhaled the scent of fresh coffee.

Coffee and books are her two favorite things.

She checked her watch. Only five more minutes until Kaya said she would meet her.

She had read an article about the accident back at the field office, but couldn't find an obituary for the siblings. She wanted to know more about the two. If Paul was asking about them, they had something to do with her past. But how could that be?

She had searched every waking hour not consumed by work for years and hadn't connected her life to the death of two young adults in Alaska.

These days she only looked over her notes on her birthday hoping and praying that she saw something that she missed before.

Tears burned the backs of her eyes. Paul clearly never stopped looking for her story. She needed to find him, sure. But deep down she also wanted to know about her parents.

Did she look like her dad or her mom?

Were they still alive? Why didn't they want her?

She needed to focus or these tears were going to burst forth and she'd need more than five minutes to put herself back together.

Nalani took her black cold brew over to the small table by the window and she sat facing the door. Exactly at their meet time, Kaya walked through the door. She greeted the barista behind the counter and asked for her usual drink order then took a seat across from Nalani.

Nalani breathed in the nutty scent of her brew rather than diving into the questions. She didn't want to scare Kaya off. "Thank you for meeting me again."

"I really am sorry to hear about your brother disappearing." Kaya relaxed into the seat.

Nalani nodded. She didn't plan to stop until she found him. Hopefully Davin also wouldn't stop looking for him. Nalani said, "I had a few other questions about Lorelai and Wyatt."

The barista came with Kaya's drink so Nalani paused.

Kaya thanked her and turned her attention back to Nalani. "Sometimes it is best to leave the past in the past."

She had already said that, but Nalani couldn't let this go. "Paul came to you about these two people. He told me that he was looking into my family. Did either of them have a child?"

Nalani's lungs stopped working as she stared at the elder woman. Sadness coated her expression. "Wyatt did not have any children. He was my brother's best friend and was always over at our house. He hadn't dated all through high school and had finally gotten the nerve to ask me out on a date the week before he died. He was a good man and a loving brother."

"What about Lorelai? Did she have any children?"

"Lorelai was a free spirit who wanted nothing to do with our traditions." Kaya sipped her drink. "She went off to college and came back seeking refuge. The elders took her in and she was finding healing again."

Was she purposely not answering the question? If she was, it could only be to hide the truth. "But did she have a baby?"

"While she was here, she did not give birth. I didn't really know her well. I was away on a research vessel when she returned. I can only tell you what was told to me."

Something in this story still did not add up.

Why was Kaya not giving her a straight story?

Maybe she should change her tactic. "Did you hear back from Lorelei's aunt?"

"I have not heard from her." Kaya shifted in her seat.

Time to cut out the middleman in order to find answers. "Would you mind giving me her address so that I can learn more about their family?"

Kaya pulled back from the table and her gaze darted away. When she turned back to Nalani there was uncertainty in their depths. "Joyce prefers to be alone. I'm not sure that she'll want to speak with you. Or anyone for that matter."

She stared at her coffee cup, but Nalani waited, praying this woman would help her.

Kaya sighed as she stood. "I will call her now."

Nalani doubted the woman had called her before, even if she said she had.

Kaya pinned her with a stern look. "But I warn you painful memories are not an easy thing to bare. She may refuse to talk about them."

Nalani nodded her head. She knew all too well about painful memories. Her childhood was full of them. If there was one thing that she and this woman had in common it would be sorrow.

Kaya walked to the far end of one of the bookshelves to place the call. When she returned, the grim line of her lips made Nalani's stomach tighten.

"She said she will speak with you, but only if you bring a blueberry scone and listen to the story without interrupting."

That was great news, so why was Kaya still frowning?

Nalani pushed that errant thought to the side. "Thank you."

Kaya pulled a piece of paper from her bag, wrote down the address, and handed it to Nalani. Before letting go Kaya lowered her voice, "Joyce is an elder of my people. If she asks you to leave, please respect her enough to do so."

Nalani dipped her head in acknowledgement. She wasn't going to badger the poor woman.

She only wanted answers, and this grieving aunt was the closest she'd come to them her entire life.

Kaya grabbed her bag and left Nalani sitting there. She watched the woman's retreating back. That was the strangest conversation she'd had in a while, and she wasn't sure if she had learned anything new.

Except that she now just might have a living relative that could maybe, just maybe answer her questions instead of talking around them.

Would it lead her to Paul?

*Lord, I hope I find him down this path I'm on.*

The air off the bay swirled around her as she stepped from the cafe, bringing the salt smell of the ocean with it. She loved that smell. Pausing in front of her car, she looked out over Resurrection Bay. The dark waters were unsettled today. Boats bobbed up and down not minding the small waves that broke the serenity of the surface.

She breathed in deep wanting the sea air to fortify her before facing Joyce. A strong arm snaked around her neck and another around her waist.

Before she could think, her feet were lifted off the ground and Nalani was dragged backward.

He was carrying her.

And the docks were getting further away.

She tried to scream but the arm around her throat squeezed her windpipe so tightly that she couldn't breathe.

"Leave the past alone." Hot breath whispered past her ear. "Go home. Next time won't be a warning."

"FBI! Let her go!"

At the shout, the man released her.

She hit the ground hard and tumbled to her hands and knees. Nalani sucked in as much air as she could manage when two black booted feet topped with black slacks came into view.

The person crouched down and she looked into the eyes of Mr. FBI himself.

Davin. "Are you OK?"

She could only nod. The fire in her throat made her want to gulp down a gallon of water to smooth the rough edges away.

Davin placed his hand on her upper arm to steady her. "I'll call—"

"Go." She shook her head. "Catch that guy."

Davin paused only a moment before taking off in the direction the man had run.

Nalani sat on the concrete and laid her head against the wooden siding of the building. Her hands shook with adrenaline. Nalani prayed her thanks to God that Davin had found her before something worse could have happened.

She took a few deep breaths to make sure her lungs were going to work correctly.

Davin came back around the corner, a thunderous look on his face. "He jumped in a gray truck and got away. I couldn't see the license because mud covered most of the plate." He stepped closer to her. "Are you actually okay?"

This close she could see the streaks of gray in his blue eyes. "I'm fine now that I can breathe again."

He scowled and helped her to her feet. She rubbed her neck. Everything was sore. Some lemon tea with honey was something she could use right now. But she was supposed to be meeting with Joyce right now.

"Did he say anything to you?"

Nalani winced. "He told me to leave the past alone and go home." She swallowed and it felt like rubbing her hand through shards of glass. She cleared her throat. "He also said that next time wouldn't be a warning."

Davin put his hand on her lower back. "Come on. Let's get back to the office where it's safer and we can finish this conversation."

She wasn't sure if it was because of the lack of oxygen to her brain during the attack or the fear that was breaking down her walls. The strength his touch gave her made her want to give in and rely on it too much.

But she couldn't do that. It was only a matter of time before he would leave her. Or this time, she would be the one leaving. And she would be on her own. Again.

# Chapter 4

Davin got Nalani settled on the couch in their break room. He kept wondering what would have happened if he hadn't decided to follow her. He shook those thoughts away.

She was safe for now.

He placed the mug of hot water in front of her and held out the box of teas that Taylor insisted on keeping in the break room. His colleague was downstairs working on tracking down the man from the video at Paul's cabin and where the burner phone had been purchased.

Their suspect had left before Taylor had gotten to the house, but the cameras got a partial side profile of his face.

Was it the same man who shot at them earlier? Was the guy who tried to take Nalani the one and the same? Or was there more than one person coming after her?

"I figured you'd want something warm to help with your throat." He put the honey beside her cup.

"Thank you." Her hoarse voice made his protective instincts flare.

She dipped her tea bag in the hot liquid and breathed in the steam. "This is perfect." She looked at him over her mug. "Thank you for showing up when you did."

Her sincerity melted away some of the tension he held inside.

He sat beside her. "Do you remember anything else about him?"

She closed her eyes. "He was tall and muscular. His voice wasn't too deep, but held a hint of some kind of accent." She opened her eyes. "It all happened so fast. I couldn't get any more details."

He reached toward her then stopped before touching her arm. "You did a great job."

She snorted, "Hardly. I'd be passed out or dead if you wouldn't have interrupted him."

"I don't think he intended to kill you." *At least not this time,* he added to himself.

He hated to push her, but he needed to do his job. "Did he sound like the man who attacked you at Paul's cabin?"

She stared past him then shook her head slowly.

Just what he feared.

There was more than one man chasing after her.

"Given what just happened," she took another sip of tea before asking, "do you think Paul's disappearance is connected to Lorelai's and Wyatt's deaths?"

"It's clear that there is a threat against you specifically, but I can't rule out our current case. The group we are going after is dangerous. If they suspected Paul of anything close to betrayal, then he is in more trouble than just missing check-in."

"What makes this group so dangerous?" She set the mug down and turned to face him.

Their knees were almost touching, which made him all too aware of her. Of the way her high cheeks held a bit of pink in them or the coconut wafting to him, enticing him to lean closer.

He started to shake his head. He wanted to tell her all of it, but protocol was not something he broke even if it was a family member. "All I can tell you is it is a matter of national security."

She rolled her eyes. "Figures a fed would say that."

She stood and paced the small room. Her finger tapped her chin. Making her way to the far end next to the kitchen, she spun, placing her hands on her hips.

"What *can* you tell me? This is my brother. I..." She cleared her throat. "I can't lose him too."

Davin squeezed the back of his neck and let his hand fall to his side. "Two months ago when we arrested some teens, we stumbled upon a connection to this group. Neither said much and the day after someone paid their bail, they were found floating in the Kenai River." He blew out a breath and walked to stand in front of her.

"What is it?" She lifted her chin and he saw softness with the worry for her brother in her eyes.

"One of them hinted at an event happening soon. Something that would bring the correct order back to Alaska. They only mentioned one man. We learned enough about him to make connections, but we still had no idea what the event was. We needed information and Paul volunteered to go in undercover."

"That sounds like Paul. He was always first to step up when people needed saving. Do you have any better ideas of what the event is now?"

He sighed. "I can't tell you even if we did. Paul's last message said he was on to something and that he would give details at next check-in."

He watched as she began to pace again. The movement made him want to go for a run. Maybe he should suggest taking her to the gym he frequented.

A trail run was out of the question given that her life had just been threatened, but he could keep watch inside a gym. Besides, the owner was a veteran and a friend he could rely on to keep her safe.

He was about to offer it when she stopped abruptly and stomped over to stand in front of him. "I'd like to go back to Paul's cabin. I can't stay here forever, and I need to figure out what made him disappear."

There was no way he was letting her go unprotected. He still wasn't convinced that the threat against her was because of her past and not because of Spartak and the case. Maybe it was all connected. Though, he couldn't see how.

"I can't let you go unprotected around Alaska looking for answers."

She cocked her head to the side. "Great. So, you'll help me find answers and get Paul back?"

"There is a clear threat against you. Because you are Paul's sister, I won't let you go unprotected." He chose his next words carefully. "I will continue to search for Paul and the threat against the US."

She relaxed her shoulders a bit, but not much. "I would appreciate that, but I'm going to continue to look into what Paul found out about my past. I can't quite shake the feeling that it's connected to all of this "

"What do you mean?" A rock sat in his stomach. What hadn't she told him?

She blew out a breath and flopped back on the couch. "Paul took this assignment because he wanted a change of pace. He thought the remote field office would get him away from the crime he had experienced in Chicago."

"Okay." Paul had told him a similar thing when he hired him.

She ran her hand over her face, "When he called to mention he was looking into my past, he was already undercover. At least, according to your timetable. Whatever sent him down this rabbit hole? It happened while he was undercover."

That rock in Davin's stomach turned to ash and made his mouth dry out.

What exactly had Paul seen to make that connection? What did Nalani's past have to do with Spartak? Whatever the connection, it wouldn't be a good thing. The threat against Nalani just grew exponentially.

"Were you able to get into Paul's computer?" Her question pulled him back into focus.

He cleared his throat. "Let's go find out." Taylor's program should have worked by now.

As they descended the stairs, Davin ran through the possibilities for connections. Nalani said that she knew nothing of her birth parents. Did she not have a birth certificate? He would have to look back over the profile Taylor ran on her, but he also wanted to hear what she knew herself.

"Do you have names for your birth parents?" He asked the question over his shoulder as they stepped into the hall.

When she didn't answer, he stopped before entering the room.

She shook her head and looked down at the floor. "I tried looking for a birth certificate in my CPS file, but there was nothing listed there. The report said that I was left on the doorstep of a fire station and was put with the Prices, my first foster home. They were the ones to give me a name."

He couldn't imagine not knowing his parents' names. His father's and mother's faces flashed before him. There were times when he didn't want to be in their shadow, but he was blessed to have both of them still in his life even, with the challenges.

He opened the door and ushered her in. "Have you tried talking with your original case worker?"

She breezed past him and took the seat she had been sitting in before leaving to meet with Kaya.

Nalani sighed. "She passed away before I could find her. I talked with her daughter, but she of course knew nothing of the girl with no name. She did promise when she went through her mother's things that she would look out for any mention of me. I haven't heard from her since."

Until he had a definitive connection between her past and Spartak, he would need to keep his focus on the current threat and keep her safe in the process.

"It's a possibility that Paul saw something that connects you to our current investigation, but it is also a possibility that he went dark because he needed the heat on him to cool before making contact."

It was wishful thinking and a probability that wasn't likely. She dipped her head and raised her eyebrows. "You really think that is true? Don't you have protocols for that kind of situation?"

"Yes." He took a long breath through his nose to reset his mind. "Let's see what Paul had on his computer. Maybe he left us some bread crumbs to find him."

She furrowed her eyebrows. "I didn't take you for a classic novel kind of guy."

He smirked. "I love books of all kinds. Except crime novels. I get enough of that at work." He winked and the blush that crept up her neck made his heart tick up a few notches.

Flirting with the person you were protecting never ended well.

He unplugged Paul's computer and rolled back towards her.

*Focus on the case, Schulz.*

Right now he needed to find Paul and stop Spartak.

Mr. FBI agent was more complex than she first thought. Maybe she should stop judging people based on their occupation. Paul was an agent too, but he was also her brother and not so uptight.

Maybe it was only Davin.

She hoped, though, that he missed the blush that crept up her neck at his wink. Did he do that to flirt with her or was he showing her his spunky side? Either way, she had to admit to herself she wouldn't mind seeing that side of him again, but not until she knew Paul was found.

She slid closer to him and tried not to get distracted by his woodsy aftershave. He pulled up the file history and opened the last document that Paul had been working on before he disappeared. The page was filled with notes. This would take some time to comb through and make sense of his train of thought.

Numbers and initials broke the document into sections.

She frowned. "It looks like this was some kind of log. Those numbers could be dates, but I'm not sure what the letters mean. The notes themselves don't make much sense. What can you make of it?"

The sentences talked about nothing helpful to their investigation, or so it seemed.

He leaned toward the screen and squinted as if that would somehow magically make the jumbled words make sense.

"Hmmm." That was all he said before he got up and left the room. Where was he going? He returned with a book in his hands.

"What are you..."

"Just give me a second, I think he wrote in a book cipher."

A book cipher? This was real life, not some spy novel. "Why would Paul do that?" She didn't even try to keep the skepticism from her voice.

"When you go undercover, you take extra precautions in case the worst happens. If Spartak found out where Paul was living and his computer fell into their hands, writing in a cipher would make figuring out his notes that much harder," Davin stated flatly like this was common practice. News flash, this wasn't normal. Or at least it wasn't normal for her.

She waited as patiently as her strung-out nerve endings would let her. She wanted answers, not more questions.

Finally, he sat back. "His last log said that he was meeting with a leader. It was meant to happen last night."

"That's it?" That wasn't very helpful.

"He also mentions coffee and Lysander. I'm not sure who that is."

She had heard of that name before. It was on her trip to Greece to cover the refugee camps overflowing across the countryside. People fleeing from the unrest in their native homes.

She pulled up a search engine and typed in the name. "Lysander was a Spartan naval commander who brought about the end of the Peloponnesian War. Says here that he was a great leader and warrior who took back what Sparta deemed as rightfully theirs."

Davin's spine stiffened.

"Why was that important?" she asked, focusing on his face. Looking for signs of deception.

His jaw twitched, but his face remained otherwise blank. "I think Paul was figuring out who the leader of the organization was and the motive behind the threat."

"You mean Spartak?"

He glanced at her. "I was hoping that you wouldn't have caught that slip."

She bit back a grin. "It comes with the territory of being a reporter."

He moved the computer toward himself. Anyone could feel the icy tension that settled into the room. She resisted the urge to reach out and touch his arm. The last thing she needed was for him to shut her out completely.

"I'm not here on a work assignment. I will not be writing about this story unless you give me express permission to do so." The distance went from frosty to cool breeze, but there was still doubt in his eyes.

Davin pitched his voice low. "Publishing could get Paul killed. If they haven't made him as an agent yet, then there is still hope he comes out of this alive. Printing anything might make him more of a target than he currently is." Davin's hard voice made the danger of the situation more of a reality.

Nalani narrowed her eyes. She would never do anything to endanger her brother. "And you showing up at his cabin isn't a red flag of his employment status?" Lydia, her foster mother, would be appalled at her tone right now, but the insinuation that she would do anything to get Paul killed made her blood boil.

"It could do just the opposite. We searched his house and took his computer. It looks like we are investigating him, not trying to save him." Davin ran his hand over his face with a sigh.

He had a point, but his accusation still stung.

"I would never publish something for the sake of accolades," Nalani said. "Especially if it put the life of someone else in danger."

His grunt was all she was going to get for acknowledgement. He said, "I'm going to send this off to a cryptanalyst I've worked with before. He can decipher the rest of this much quicker than I can."

He sent the document off and then opened the only other document on the computer. This one was a letter addressed to Nalani. Dread warred with her desire to see what message Paul left her.

"Do you mind if I read this first?" She kept her voice solid but calm.

Davin looked at her. His attention on her made her sit up straight. *Never let them see weakness. Confidence will get you respect and more answers.* Her journalism professor had been talking about the art of an interview, but it was sound advice for life itself.

"You know that I will also read over the letter?" he said. "It's evidence in an ongoing investigation."

She swallowed back the clog of emotion in her throat. "I know, but I'd like to read it first anyway."

Would he trust her enough to let her read it? She didn't like being on the receiving end of suspicion just because she was a journalist.

"Fine." His expression didn't change.

That one word gave her heart hope.

"But I'll be sitting right here. I can't let the chain of evidence be broken. We need to do everything by the book so that when we take down this organization, it'll stick."

She dipped her head in agreement. If Spartak were responsible for Paul's disappearance, then she wanted to make sure they couldn't get back up.

Nalani took a deep breath and began to read the letter.

*Hey Lani, I may or may not have found some answers to who your parents are. I can't tell you how I found the connection or where it might lead, but I'm praying that it will give you some answers I know you so desperately want. If you found this letter, it means something happened to me. Find the SD card in my Bible and talk with the person you find there. She will be able to tell you everything I know now. Love you, Sunshine! P*

Tears burned her eyes. She blinked to keep them from falling. Would she ever forgive herself if Paul died because of her desire to know where she came from? He didn't say in the letter that something would happen to him because of his search into her past, but she couldn't help thinking the worst.

"May I?" Davin's soft voice made a tear release from its hold and slide down her cheek. She only nodded, not knowing if she would be able to speak around the lump in her throat right now.

A soft tissue was pressed into her hand. She blinked rapidly as she raised her head. "Thank you," she whispered. "I can't help but feel like I'm the reason he disappeared."

"The letter doesn't say that. He just wanted to make sure if anything happened, you would know what he found." Davin placed his hand on her arm and gave her a gentle squeeze. "We are going to find him."

She blew out a slow breath and shoved the troublesome tears down. They would find her brother. They had to.

She couldn't even think about the alternative.

"Kaya helped me connect with Joyce, Wyatt and Lorelei's aunt. She might have some answers to why Paul was looking into the siblings' accident. I was supposed to meet up with her when that man..." She didn't want to finish the sentence.

"Would you mind if I go with you?" Davin asked in a gentle voice.

Relief flooded Nalani. It had been a long time since someone wanted to follow her on one of her adventures. And this adventure might be the most important one of her life.

"We need to stop and get a blueberry scone first."

Confusion flickered across his face.

She shrugged. "Kaya said that I needed to bring one and listen to her story without interrupting. She also said that

I should not disrespect Joyce because she was an elder of their tribe."

"I know where we can get the best blueberry scones in Alaska." He took Paul's computer over to another desk where a serious looking woman sat.

How had Nalani missed the other agent when they came down to the conference room? *Because you were distracted by a not-so-grumpy agent willing to help you find answers.*

The woman stood and stretched out her hand. "Hi, Nalani, right?"

Nalani shook her hand. Her grip was strong, but not crushing.

Davin said, "Agent Ertz, this is Nalani Price. Paul's sister."

"Nice to meet you." Taylor nodded. "Sorry it is under these circumstances. I'll finish searching the hard drive while you're gone."

Davin placed his hand on the small of her back to guide her to the back door. The feel gave her strength and made her knees want to turn to jelly.

She needed to get herself together if she was going to find her brother.

Before whoever was after her silenced the truth.

# Chapter 5

Downtown Seward crept past Nalani's window as Davin navigated through the streets. People walked from stores with bright colored fronts boasting of local artists or Alaska themed gifts. She read about the town on her flight to Anchorage. The tour book did nothing to capture the beauty of how the mountains crash into the water or the toughness of the people and the town was captured in their ability to make ends meet in such a rugged landscape.

The town stretched between the docks and downtown, but was small enough that if she wanted to she could walk just about everywhere.

Chicago's iconic skyline was big and impressive. But this place called to her.

As if it could be home.

When he pulled into a parking spot close to what looked like an old church, Nalani opened her door and spoke over the roof of the car. "We could have walked here."

Davin's head was on a swivel. "It's safer to drive. Besides, this will get us to Joyce faster since we didn't have to walk back and forth just for a blueberry scone."

She slammed her door and crossed her arms over her middle in the hopes of keeping the chill of the situation from seeping into her core.

The windows peeked around the building with simple stained glass, a nod to its history. She walked up the steps admiring the arched doorway, imagining the parsons of this town finding solace here. Maybe she could find solace in this town also.

Her breath hitched as she stepped through the door into the  art gallery. The paintings and photographs each captured a beauty that drew her in like it was part of her.

How could that be?

She'd lived and visited so many different places around the world, but there was something about the Alaskan wilderness that called to her.

"That one is my favorite." Davin nodded toward a painting of the fjords. Icebergs floated in the swirling water and a whale's tail broke the surface.

"How long have you been here in Alaska?" She wasn't sure he would answer a personal question. They had only ever talked about finding Paul, but a part of her wanted to know about this agent.

"I was born and raised in Anchorage. Seward was a favorite spot for us to vacation in the summer time. Dad and

I would rent out a boat and fish the silver salmon run every year." A whisper of a smile brushed across his lips. One that made her wish she had good memories of family. The familiar feeling of loneliness washed over her.

The VanKirks made her feel welcome, but she's never had blood relatives in her life.

When she looked back toward Agent Schulz, he was studying her. "I didn't mean to upset you."

Here she thought she still had her mask in place. "I'm fine. Let's go get the scone and hopefully some answers."

He opened his mouth as if he wanted to say something, but closed it quickly, then motioned for her to follow him.

Davin approached the small woman behind the counter. "Pauline, do you still have a blueberry scone for the day?"

The woman with salt-and-pepper hair pulled into a neat bun smiled at him. "It's your day. I have one left."

Nalani reached for her wallet, but Davin's hand on hers stopped her. Her arm tingled at his touch. "I've got this. Would you like anything?"

The cinnamon rolls looked divine, but the butterflies in her stomach made her doubt she'd be able to keep them down. He followed her gaze and asked Pauline for the last two cinnamon rolls.

"You didn't have to do that," she whispered, not trusting her voice to be solid.

His lips hitched to one side. "It is my pleasure. I only allow myself to come here on special occasions. Unlike Paul, who ate one of these every morning..." His words trailed off and he spun on his heels back to the counter. "Pauline, when was the last time you saw Paul?"

Pauline tilted her head and tapped her finger on her chin. "You know, I haven't seen him the last few days. I believe it was four days ago, which is unusual for him. I figured he was traveling or something."

"Did he seem off to you that morning?"

She frowned. "He was a bit quiet that morning and he sat over there instead of leaving. Ten minutes later a young man came in and sat with him. I couldn't hear anything they were saying, but that guy gave me the creeps."

"How so?" Nalani took a step closer. She ignored the side eye that Davin tossed her way.

"He just looked like he didn't get enough love as a child, and he hated the world."

Nalani winced. People could've said the same thing about her, but she tried not to hate the whole world. Only the ones that did unspeakable evil.

"Do you have any security cameras?" Davin asked.

Pauline's eyes widened. "Is Paul alright?"

"He's missing and we are trying to find him." Nalani put as much pleading in her voice as she could without sounding too desperate.

Pauline gasped and pressed her hand to her chest, "I'll go have Trevor pull the footage for you."

Davin waited for Pauline to move out of earshot and turned to her. "Let me take lead, please. I need all the evidence to hold up in the courts."

"I need my brother back in one piece," she gritted between her clenched jaw. She usually didn't lose her cool, but this man made her insides melt. He also brought out the fierce side in her.

He leaned his head toward her. "I want him back too. But I also want to put these people in jail so that they can't come after you or him ever again."

His reminder of the threat against her splashed cold water on the fire inside. She huffed a sigh. "Fine."

She knew he was right, but it didn't make it any easier to leave the questions to someone else.

Pauline came out and handed Davin a USB drive. He took the bag of pastries and thanked her for willingly giving him the video. He put his hand on Nalani's back again and a different kind of fire smoldered at his touch.

What was it about this man that made her unable to control her own emotions? She had learned long ago to school her emotions and just disappear into the background. It kept people from noticing you and made it easier to leave when it was time.

They both got into his SUV and he offered her a cinnamon bun. "Let me send this to Agent Ertz to see if she can get a clear shot of the man."

She wanted to see the video herself now, but she also wanted to go see Joyce. "Promise to share the photo with me, if she gets a clear shot?"

"Promise." He pulled out a small tablet and sent the video file off.

"Thank you. Let's go see if Joyce has any answers for us."

Davin took the road the opposite direction of Paul's cabin along the bay. The cliffs dropped down to the road and then straight into the sea. There wasn't much of a beach or shoreline. It only added to the rugged wilderness of the area.

"Do you know anything about Lowell Point?" If the man had grown up relatively close by, he'd know more about the area.

"It was a homestead of Franklin Lowell, who had married an Aleut woman named Mary. She was one of the first native peoples to return to the Resurrection Bay area after the Russians sold Alaska to the US in the mid-1800s. She eventually sold her homesteading rights to what is now the town of Seward."

"I thought Alaska only became a state in the 1950's?"

"It did, but it was a US territory before that."

Interesting. She would need to research the history of the area more, especially before she submitted her interest story about the natives in this region.

He turned off the road and traveled part of the way up the mountain. A small cabin with smoke curling from the chimney came into view through the thick forest. She itched to find a camera and capture the serenity before her. She could only hope that the woman would have answers for her that gave her as much peace as the quaint cabin on the mountainside.

Nalani let out a breath as she silently prayed that this wouldn't be another dead end. *Lord, Mom VanKirk says that you hear me. Please give us answers.*

Davin walked behind her up the path lined with wildflowers. The scent of them would normally entice her to stop and take photos, but questions and nervous energy kept her from really seeing their beauty today.

The boards on the steps creaked under her weight and set her heart beating faster. Could this woman really be her great-aunt? She rapped lightly on the door.

Shuffling from inside preceded the door cracking open. A small woman shorter than Nalani's five foot four frame peered out. Her eyes widened and her bony fingers covered her mouth. "Who are you?" Her hoarse voice quivered.

Nalani took a breath, then said, "I was hoping that you could help me figure that out. I've come to learn about Lorelai."

"I knew God would bring you home." A tear slid down the woman's weathered face. "Come in, my child. I have much to tell you."

The small cabin didn't have much in the way of seating unless he wanted to sit close to Nalani on the love seat. As much as his heart lifted at the possibility his brain won out and he stood next to her leaning against the back of the sofa.

Joyce took the rocking chair closer to the fireplace with a lap blanket draped over the arm rest. The worn look on her face hinted of the long years she'd lived.

Joyce sipped the tea from her mug. Nalani wrapped hers in her hands and stared at the liquid inside.

"You look just like her." The elder's voice shook. She set the mug down and reached for a book underneath the end table. She opened it to a page and ran her fingers over the page before giving it to Nalani.

A gasp escaped her and tears gathered in her eyes. Davin leaned over her shoulder and scanned the page of photos. When his gaze landed on one of two teens smiling widely, his own breath hitched. The young lady looked almost exactly like Nalani.

"Lorelai was always a free spirit. She could turn anyone's day around. That was until after the summer she turned eighteen."

"What happened?" Nalani whispered so quietly he wasn't sure if Joyce could hear her.

"That summer she volunteered at her best friend's place to train sled dogs and care for the new puppy litter. She loved that job." A ghost of a smile lifted her lips. "Their farm was close to Cooper's Landing and that summer they were regrading the highway along the mountains. He was on the crew. They fell in love. I remember Helen telling me about it. Helen would have been your grandmother. She was worried that Lorelai would have her heart broken at the end of the summer when he moved on with the crew."

Joyce sighed. "Nothing could dim Lorelai's brightness, though. She seemed to be hopeful that he would come back to find her. That their love would conquer the distance." Joyce sighed again and unshed tears glistened in her eyes. "When she discovered she was pregnant, she tried reaching out to him, but his father told her to never contact him again."

"Who was he?" Nalani asked.

Joyce looked into the fireplace as if seeing a time long ago. "She only ever called him Nick."

"What happened to her? To her baby?" Nalani twisted her fingers in her lap.

He wanted to reach out to give her comfort, but he wasn't sure she would receive his touch and he needed to keep his distance. He had an agent to find. Her brother.

"A week after she was told to stay away from Nick, she noticed someone watching her. When she came out of the doctor's office in Anchorage, a man attempted to kidnap her." Joyce dabbed her eyes with a handkerchief. "Thank goodness Wyatt was there. After that Lorelai stayed with me and we had a midwife come to my house. She went through her weeks excited, and a little scared to be a single mother. I believed she was scared of Nick's father also. She believed he was the one behind the attempted kidnapping."

Davin could feel the tension rolling off of Nalani's shoulders. He reached over and gave her hand a gentle squeeze. Nalani looked at him and he could see she was barely holding back her tears. The sight made him want to find her grandfather and find out why a man would try to kidnap a pregnant teenage girl.

"You brought joy back to her. When she held you it was like seeing the old Lorelai. The night you were born, she made me promise that if anything happened to her I would keep you a secret. To keep you safe."

"You were the one that dropped me off on the steps of the fire station in Chicago?" Nalani swallowed hard.

That was a detail he hadn't expected. He knew she had been raised in foster care, but there was clearly more to it than what he expected. But could this all be connected to Paul's disappearance?

Davin needed to work Paul's disappearance like an FBI agent, not a man drawn to a woman he couldn't have, helping her find who she was.

"There aren't many places to hide a child in Alaska. I went to a place I thought you could hide." Joyce rocked slowly and stared at her niece, "I prayed for you everyday."

Tears pooled in both women's eyes, and he felt the burn in his own throat. Nalani flew out of her seat and kneeled next to her great-aunt. She laid her head in the elder's lap while Joyce stroked her silky hair.

When Nalani sat back on her feet, her words flowed quickly from her. "I have so many questions, but I have to know. Why would someone threaten me to keep me from learning who my parents were?"

Joyce stiffened her spine. "Did someone follow you here?" She turned her sharp eyes to Davin and continued, "You need to protect her. I can't lose the only family I have left."

Davin swallowed. He didn't want to make promises he couldn't keep, but the look in the woman's eyes had him speaking without thinking. "I will do everything I can to keep her safe. Can you tell us if you've ever met with FBI agent Paul VanKirk?"

Davin dug out his phone and pulled up a picture of Paul.

He showed her the screen, but Joyce shook her head. "I have never seen him before."

Nalani stood next to him now, "Can you tell us anything else about my father?"

"Even if I knew more, I'm not sure it's a wise idea to know more." Shadows under Joyce's eyes became more pronounced and her shoulders drooped. As if the whole exchange had taken all of her energy.

Davin placed his hand on the small of Nalani's back and leaned toward her. "We should let her rest."

Nalani started to shake her head, but paused when Joyce's eyes began to drift shut.

"We're going to let you rest, Joyce." Nalani said.

She kneeled again in front of her and took Joyce's hand. "Please do what you need to to keep yourself safe. I will be back to swap more stories." She gave the older woman a hug and placed the lap blanket over her.

A hint of a smile brushed across the old woman's face. She signed as if a weight had been lifted from her.

Nalani stood and brushed past Davin.

"Thank you for talking with us." He left his business card on the coffee table. "Please call me if you see anything suspicious." Even if she didn't hear him because she'd already drifted off, she would see his card when she awoke.

By the time he emerged from the cabin, Nalani was sitting in the front seat of the SUV, a blank stare on her face. He climbed into the driver's seat, but didn't turn the vehicle on. Instead, he turned to face her. "Do you need to talk about anything?"

"You mean like the fact that my mother is dead, most likely because my grandfather ordered her killed?" There was a hardness in her voice, but her eyes betrayed her fear.

"We don't know that for sure." They had no proof the accident wasn't more than what it seemed on the surface.

She scowled at him. "But it has merit. You've gotten more answers than Paul got looking into who I am."

Davin wasn't sure that was true. They had no idea what Paul had learned or why he disappeared.

Nalani continued. "The question we need to ask is, did this family take him to stop him from finding the truth or did something happen with the investigation?"

"I would have said it was Spartak, but now I have no idea." He scratched his chin.

"I wish that Paul were here. He would know what to do."

For the second time he reached out to her and this time his hand rested on her arm. The touch threatened his resolve to keep things professional between them. Why did his heart want him to take this feisty woman in his arms and tell her that he could be her rock? He didn't even know her all that well beyond the report that Ertz pulled. But the more he learned, the more spending time with her threatened his resolve to focus only on his career.

"We will find him, Nalani." His soft voice made her bring her gaze to his.

"But what if it's too late." Her chin began to quiver. "They killed my mother. What would keep them from killing my brother too?"

No words or platitudes could satisfy the truth in her words. He would not stop working this case until Paul was found. Dead or alive. For Nalani's sake, he hoped Paul was alive.

Davin's phone vibrated with a text. He picked it up instead of answering her question. *Got something off video. Found photos on computer.* Ertz's text gave him a bit of hope.

Maybe they could find Paul.

Preferably alive.

# Chapter 6

Nalani's words haunted him as Davin drove them back to the field office. Could it be possible that the same people who killed her mother had also killed Paul? If they were responsible for Lorelai's death, they had made it look like an accident. Paul was a federal agent, which meant that killing him outright would draw unnecessary attention to themselves.

Had they discovered Paul's true identity?

Still, killing him and hiding the body wasn't their MO in the past. There was still a better chance that he was simply kidnapped. Or, at least Davin's heart was trying to convince his head of that reality. Not only because it meant his agent was alive.

But Nalani would get her brother back.

They would rescue Paul.

Either way, there was a terror threat looming which he still didn't know much about and he had an agent missing. They needed answers and soon.

As he pulled into his spot behind the historic building, he turned to her. "Ertz says she found something on the video. Will you like to join us before you dive more into Lorelai and Nick?"

"Absolutely. And, Davin." This time she reached out to him and heat fled up his arm at her touch. "Thank you." As quickly as she made contact, she withdrew her hand and got out of the car.

He gave himself a mental shake. He needed to stay focused on the case, not on how she made his heart kick up a few notches. He muttered to himself, "There's a terror threat, get yourself together."

With that pep talk he got out of the car and punched in the security code to let them both in. Ertz stood as they walked into the office space and nodded toward the conference room.

Once they were all settled, she put a picture up on the screen. "This lovely peach of a human was the one who met with Paul the day he disappeared.'

A grainy picture of a bald man with a tattoo wrapped around his neck and descending underneath his shirt. He could only imagine the amount of tats across the man's body.

"Do you have an identity?" Davin asked. Nalani leaned forward and bunched her eyebrows together.

"Meet Ian Volkov. Son of Alexei Volkov, Russian businessman who is suspected of nefarious dealings, but nothing seems to stick to his slick suit." Ertz put a picture of Alexei up on the board. The man looked as smooth as a salesman convincing a widow to give up all of her savings to a new endeavor.

Davin watched Nalani, but there was no flicker of recognition.

Davin turned back to Ertz. "What do we know about Ian?"

"I'm still digging. Russia isn't exactly forthcoming with criminal records with the US, but he hasn't been dinged by Interpol."

"Play the video of their meeting." Davin needed to see Paul's reaction to the man so he could see if there were any clues as to what they'd talked about. Davin dared a glance at Nalani. She was staring at the picture of Ian.

"How tall is he?" She looked at him and then at Ertz.

"Based on how tall Paul is," Ertz shrugged one shoulder, "I would guess about six or six one? Why?"

"That was about the height of the man that tried to take me at the coffee shop today."

"Someone tried to take you?" Ertz snapped her head toward him and he saw the accusation there.

He raised his hands before he responded. "I was going to tell you about our adventures after you were done showing us what you found."

Ertz huffed, but continued. "I'm working on finding more about Ian and Alexei. If we can find dad we might be able to find the son. I also found an article about an up-coming critical minerals summit in Fairbanks and satellite photos of the Chugach National Forest, Kenai National

Park, and some of the islands in Resurrection Bay hidden on Paul's hard drive. I'm not sure where he got the photos or how old they are. Just beginning my metadata dive into the files."

"You said hidden on Paul's hard drive?" Nalani tilted her head, a move he was beginning to associate with her ability to sort through details.

"Yes. He hid the folder so that if someone did a quick search of his files they wouldn't show up. He also placed an encryption on the folder, which is what took me so long to get inside."

Nalani slowly turned to him. He could see all of the questions that wanted to burst out, but she simply stared at him.

"So you think these photos and summit have something to do with his assignment?" she finally asked.

His mind screamed *yes*, but he simply stated, "Possibly."

"I see. Then I will let you both look into that while I figure out who killed my mother."

Ertz's eyebrows winged up, but before she could ask any questions a voice called from the storefront. "Hello?"

The two agents shared a glance then Ertz slipped out to the storefront through the false door that looked like a bookcase in an office out front. The building was a historical site in downtown Seward. They set the front portion up as a nod to the building's original owners.

The front was only open on the weekends when volunteers could be out front to answer questions about the town. Since it was Thursday, the appearance of someone out there set him on edge.

"Nalani, grab your bag and computer. We're heading upstairs."

Nalani looked at him with a curious stare, but grabbed her things without argument. Once they were upstairs with the door locked she let the question fly.

"Care to share *why* we are barricading ourselves up here?"

"The 'storefront,'" he used air quotes, "is only opened on the weekends to the public. It's staffed with volunteers who have been vetted, telling people about life in Seward long ago."

"So, having some random person out there during the week isn't a normal thing?" She crossed her arms.

He shook his head slowly. Nor should it ever have happened. That front door was always kept locked and had a security code attached to it as well. Davin sat and brought up the security feed. Ertz talked with the family of three pointing to different things on display.

He needed to figure out why the door had been unlocked. He pulled up the security log and scanned through the last several entries. There among the records logged of the back door security codes was Paul's specific code inputted in the front room.

"Paul."

"What?" Nalani spun around.

Davin pulled up the camera footage for the front room again and went back to the timestamp matching the code entry. A man about the same build as Paul entered with his hat pulled low on his head and hood up. He placed something in one of the vases on the shelf then left.

"Is that Paul? It could be him, but I didn't see his face." Nalani's words made his spine stiffen and he turned his computer away from her.

"Sorry," she said. "You just didn't reply and the look on your face said this was super important."

He relaxed his shoulders a bit. "I was just checking to see why the front door was unlocked. I think Paul tried to get us a message two days ago."

"So he knew he was going to be taken?" She scrunched her face with disbelief. "Why wouldn't he tell me?"

"Believe it or not, this is a good thing. If he suspected he had been made, he would have gone dark. He would have immediately gotten rid of his phone and anything else that could have been tracked."

"Which includes texting your little sister to let her know you wouldn't be in touch for a few days. Then where would he go?"

Davin half grinned. "Knowing Paul, he would have tried to keep collecting evidence."

"But couldn't that get him captured or...." She stared at the floor.

Neither of them wanted to say it, but if Paul had already been made and he was found, he was a dead man.

"Wait." She stepped toward him, invading his space with her coconut scent. "Why would he risk coming here? If he went dark, coming here would put him at risk, right?"

It was a question he had asked himself. "Maybe. Not many people know that the back half of this building is an FBI field office." *If he was being followed, then we might catch them on our security feed.* "We need to see what message he left us."

As soon as the family stepped out the door, Davin closed his computer and motioned for Nalani to follow him. Silently they descended the stairs into the office the same time that Ertz appeared through the hidden door.

"Who in the world left that door open?" Ertz set her hands on her hips.

"Paul did." At the mention of their fellow agent, Ertz's tirade died. "Stay here and watch over Nalani while I get the note."

Nalani began to protest, but he strode across the room and out the door before she had time to get more than one word out.

The sounds of Ertz running interference filtered through the air before the door closed again. His team may not have been together long, but they had each other's back.

Now, to see what clue Paul had left them.

Davin walked over to the delicate hand painted vase from the 1920's. He gripped the folded paper and slid his hand out. There was nothing written on the outside and the only words scrawled inside were, "C U THERE" and was signed CF.

This had to mean something.

Now to try and put all of the pieces together.

"Is he always like this?" Nalani blew at a strand of hair that fell out of her messy bun.

Taylor chuckled. "You mean all business and no play? Or overprotective?"

"The second one." Because she had seen a bit of a playful side already.

Taylor sighed this time. "He has always felt that he needed to prove himself worthy of his last name, but I wouldn't want to work with any other senior agent. Your life is in danger. He's going to do everything he can to keep you safe."

*Who exactly are his parents?*

The question was on the tip of her tongue when Davin walked in with his lips pursed. Should she ask why he felt he needed to prove himself?

"What did the note say?" The question flew from her lips without stopping at her brain's filter first.

Davin's head snapped up and he hesitated.

"Right. Open case. Never mind." She picked up her computer and headed toward the conference room.

Davin followed her and sat beside her. She waited for her laptop to come back to life so she could get back to figuring out who killed her mother and uncle. She had wanted a family all her life. Now that she knew they were gone, she'd find the truth. She always did.

"You're right. This is part of an open investigation, but you also know Paul the best of all of us. If I show you the note, you cannot ask about how it is connected to our active case."

She wasn't sure to be excited that he trusted her enough to share or hurt that he had to preempt that trust with an unspoken threat. "I just want my brother back."

Davin unfolded the paper and sat it between them. "What do you make of this note?"

She leaned toward the scrap of paper and read the brief note. "It's definitely Paul's hand writing, but..." She stared at the letters.

"But?" Davin encouraged her to continue.

"But I've never known him to use text speech even when he sends an actual text message." She pulled out her phone and showed him the text channel she had with her brother. "See? Whole sentences. Grammar. Punctuation. He knows my love of proper English." She waited until he looked at her again. "So the question we need to ask is why he would write C U instead of writing out the phrase?"

Davin's eyes sparkled as a grin spread across his lips. He snapped his fingers and stood quickly. "That's it."

"What's it?" His excitement made her smile, but she was still confused.

"You gave me an idea and possibly the reason behind the terror attack. Now to figure out where and when." He bent forward and kissed her cheek. Then drew very still only inches from her face.

The next beat, he retreated so quickly through the conference door that it took her a moment to realize he was gone.

The touch of his lips on her skin lingered and it did strange things to her heart. Her head knew not to hope that there was something there between them. But her love deprived heart was winning the battle.

She laid her hand against her cheek hoping she could keep the heat from leaving her. If only that gesture was real and not a reaction born out of excitement.

She watched him make his way towards Agent Ertz's desk where they talked in hushed tones. Who was she kidding? She'd never belonged in any place before except for the apartment she rented in Chicago. It was small but it was hers. *Was that all you wanted, an apartment and an editor who hardly appreciates your work?*

After spending only a day with Special Agent Davin Schulz, she wasn't sure what her answer would be anymore.

Could she really move to Alaska permanently?

She tore her eyes away from the handsome agent and refocused her efforts on finding who killed her mother.

Although figuring that out might be more difficult than she'd hoped. If the police back then had deemed it an accident, what were the chances she could find enough evidence almost 30 years later to get the answers she wanted?

Nalani drummed her fingers along the edge of her laptop. "Let's assume that Granddad killed Mom. Then I should start with dear ol' Dad. He just might be the link that would help me connect everything."

Sometimes when she was trying to crack a story she would talk the details out loud. She stole a glance toward the two agents in the office. They were busy with whatever idea Davin had had.

She pulled up a search engine on her screen and typed in *Nick Coopers Landing*. What were the chances that her father still lived in Coopers Landing? Joyce's words came back to her.

He was on a work crew fixing the road and she was certain that he didn't stick around after the summer. Could he have been in college at the time? That would put him in his 50s or later now.

She tapped her finger against her chin. It was a long shot but right now she would grab at any straw thrown her way.

She walked to the door and cleared her throat. Davin and Taylor both looked her way with a strange expression on their faces. "We'll get to those looks in a second, but I have a question to ask. A favor, actually."

Davin stood straight and gave her his full attention, "I'll try my best to make it work."

How she wished those words meant more than they did. "Do you know if there would be any records of the people working on the roadways or any way to figure out which company was in charge of a project?"

"Well, the company would have records of their crews, but I'm not sure how long they keep those records."

Nalani liked that she didn't have to tell him the train of her thoughts. That he instinctively knew where she was going with this line of questioning. It was like he understood her. Something so few people did.

Davin tilted his head. "As for who did which project, the municipality should have public records of who won the bids for road work. Most of those have been digitized. At least that's what I've been told."

"Why didn't I think of that? Thanks, Davin." She smiled at him.

The returning grin made her want to close the distance and return his cheek kiss with a real one. Her eyes flickered to his lips and she touched her cheek.

Taylor coughed and hid her mouth behind her hand. Nalani dropped her hand and spun to begin the search for her father when Taylor's excited voice stopped her.

"I've found him!"

Nalani was across the space and shoulder to shoulder with Davin trying to see what was on the screen. Nalani's breath hitched when Paul walked across the street toward where the camera was located.

"Where is this?" she could only whisper, as if speaking any louder would somehow make him disappear.

"This is the camera at the harbor master building. It looks like he is headed to the Kenai National Park Visitor Center." Taylor stopped the footage and started typing on her screen.

Nalani just stared, not really seeing anything, only replaying her brother just walking across the street without a care in the world.

"When was this?" Taylor ignored her question so she repeated herself louder the second time.

Taylor turned to face her. "This was footage from two days ago. Davin finding Paul on our feed gave me the idea to search the public cameras from that point onward to see if we could find him. Since Seward doesn't have traffic cams, or red lights for that matter, I was limited in my scope, but I think Paul knew where the cameras were and wanted us to find him here."

Nalani straightened. "We need to go to the visitor center."

"No, you need to stay here where Agent Ertz can protect you."

Mama Lydia would not be proud of the sneer on her face right now, but this man was outside his mind if he thought he could command her to stay. "I will either go with you and *you* can protect me or I'm going on my own."

She was gearing up for a fight when Davin said, "Fine, but, Ertz, you are coming with us and if anything feels off, you take her to the safe house."

The intense agent nodded once in agreement and pulled out a handgun from her desk.

Nalani prayed that they would find another clue as to where Paul was. They had to be getting closer.

She wasn't sure how many more hits her heart could take.

# Chapter 7

Davin, Nalani, and Taylor walked into the visitor's center which sat right next to the docks. The group passed the welcome desk to the back area with a door marked for employees only. Without hesitation Davin pushed through and was greeted with rows of cubicles. Their entrance drew the attention of two park rangers in the space.

"Hey! You can't be back here." The taller ranger approached them. His lean face bore a scowl and he strode toward them, ready to throw them out.

Davin glanced at Nalani. What was he thinking bringing a civilian along to run down another lead? He had always prided himself on thinking clearly and doing everything by the book. This woman had him wanting to put her in a safe house so that no evil found her. He should do just that because his team depended on him to be at his best. Distractions could mean a good man losing his life.

Davin pulled out his ID. "I'm Davin Schulz, FBI. This is Special Agent Ertz and Ms. Price. We need to see your surveillance feeds from two days ago."

"Do you have a warrant for the footage?" The man crossed his arms and stood only a few feet from Davin. His muscles pulled at the sleeves of the park issued tan shirt.

Davin didn't want this to become a power struggle, but they needed to close in on Paul's whereabouts.

"One of my agents went missing and he was last seen on public cameras two days ago, heading towards this visitor center." At the mention of the missing agent the ranger's posture relaxed a bit.

"Let me see what I can find." He walked toward a small room off to the side of the cubicles. "What time of day am I looking for?" he asked over his shoulder.

"Two days ago around 1400 hours." Davin shifted his weight while the man typed and said a silent prayer that they would be able to get something from this trip.

They all watched the screen, no one daring to move. When Paul's large frame came through the door on the screen, adrenaline started pumping through his veins.

Nalani leaned even closer. Her nearness made it hard for him to focus on the screen in front of him.

"That's him," she said pointing at the feed. "Can you follow him?"

They watched as Paul talked with the ranger at the welcome desk then handed over his backpack. He causally walked around the displays and made his way to the back door that led out to the docks.

Paul opened the door and stopped. A man matching him in build grabbed his arm. Paul pushed him away, but the man said something which made Paul put up his hands. They watched as Paul's jaw tightened, but walked away without resistance.

Before they both disappeared from view, the bottom part of the man's face came into view through the open door.

"Freeze it there." Davin pointed. "Look familiar?"

Nalani squinted her eyes and Ertz grunted. "Scar face took Paul," Taylor said flatly.

"Why didn't Paul put up a fight? He could have easily defended himself." Nalani's confused expression made him want to right every wrong that had ever happened to her.

He placed his hand on her shoulder. "There could have been many reasons like endangering innocents around him. But I think Paul wanted to be taken."

She sucked in a breath. "Why would he want to do that?"

Davin looked at the ranger in the room with them. "Can we go someplace private?"

"You can use our conference room right next to this one." He pointed over his shoulder.

"Thanks." Davin closed the door quietly then leaned toward Nalani. "Paul is a smart agent. One of the best. If he came here, it was for a purpose. We know now that he's been sending us clues. We just need some time to put it all together."

"While you take your time, his life could be ending." Her outburst didn't surprise him, but the angst in her voice made every part of him want to fix it for her.

"I know this is hard, but we are doing everything we can."

She wiped at the stray tear that escaped her eye then took a step back, putting distance between them. "We should go get his backpack. He might have left us another clue."

Davin looked up at Ertz. She would secure the evidence. "We need to get you back to the office."

Nalani was shaking her head. "What we need to do is keep going. I'm in a ranger station in the middle of town. This is just as safe as your office."

There were so many reasons why the FBI field office was safer than the national park visitor center, but the desperation straining her voice made him reconsider.

Davin placed his hand on her arm. "Let's see what is in the pack he left for us. Then we'll make a plan."

She exhaled and some of the rigid tension in her shoulders eased out.

Ertz came back into the room and Davin dropped his hand. Nalani took a step back from him. Taylor looked between them before putting the bag on the table. Nothing happened between the two of them, but that didn't stop the flush creeping up his neck.

Davin opened the bag. He lifted out Paul's badge and some kind of wooden box. It looked like a simple cube with three different types of wood glued together on each side. It was polished and smooth.

He tucked the badge back inside. Paul had most likely left it behind in case Spartak searched his place. Just another precaution that pointed to this being less of a kidnapping and more that he was still working the undercover operation.

Davin turned the box over in his hands. It looked like one of the puzzle boxes a local artist was known to create which were sold at the stores downtown.

"May I see it?" Nalani's soft voice surprised him at its nearness.

When he looked out of the corner of his eye, he confirmed just how close she was. At this distance her hair brushed past his shoulder, making his fingers itch to run through the dark strands to discover how soft it really was.

"Sure." He handed it to her.

"Paul had sent me one like this at Christmas as a gift." She turned the box over, but he wasn't sure what she was looking for. "He sent it to me with a note letting me know he had arrived in Alaska. I don't keep anything actually in mine, but I do know how to open them."

In a fluid motion she pushed the pieces into place. She pressed a spot on the side of the box. When the lid released a satisfied look flashed across her face.

Inside was a micro SD card, like the kind that could be put into a phone to increase the storage space.

Davin picked up the small chip and gave it to Taylor who held open a small envelope. She would do her due diligence to secure the information on it and make sure it didn't fall into the wrong hands.

"You know, I've been thinking about the note that Paul left us." Nalani pulled his attention from the chip to her. "What if the C U were initials?"

That morning's discovery scrolled through his mind. Ertz and he ran through possible contacts they had to Spartak, but none of the known associates had the initials C U. When they found the article on Paul's computer, it was Ertz that suggested it had to do with the periodic table and not a person.

"They could be, but we were thinking it has more to do with minerals."

Her eyes widened. "The critical minerals summit article that Agent Ertz found. What was the article about?"

Ertz leaned against the table. "Since there is a push toward electric vehicles, the government is looking for resources inside our borders to help reduce the cost and dependency on other countries to make the new technology."

Nalani sat on the edge of the conference table opposite from Ertz. "So Paul believes that copper has something to do with this Spartak group. That explains the first initials, but what about the CF?"

"That's what I've been trying to figure out." He decided to share his thoughts with her. "We were thinking it could be the initials of the boss or the place where they're meeting."

"Could you pull up a map with all the businesses or a list of businesses in Seward? Or do you think that they were going to meet someplace else?"

He could get used to her rapid fire questions. He felt like they just might be unravelling this mess.

"Good idea." He came to stand close to her as she pulled up the map app on her phone

"There's none with the initials CF." She dropped her phone. Her eyes widened when she looked up. He should take a step back, but he couldn't make his feet move.

"Maybe it's referring to the person he was supposed to meet," he said, breaking the spell he had on her.

She started to pace to the far end of the room. The room wasn't that large and only had one large table in the center. When she reached the wall she spun back around.

"Lysander," Nalani whispered.

Davin frowned. "I've been running through our list of known members in Spartak. None of them have ever used the codename Lysander."

Ertz had her tablet out and was working on something when she gasped. "I thought so."

"What is it?" Davin went over to look at her screen.

"Scarface is Ian. I was able to get the park rangers to send me a screen grab while you guys were in here. I ran it through a program to compare the scars. There is enough visible to get a probable match."

"How much is probable?" Davin could follow a lead on a hunch, but a judge would need more to sign off on a warrant.

"Above 90% match. It's not enough for a close and shut, but it'll be a good support piece."

Ian Volkov had taken Paul.

Now to figure out where.

Her journalism brain was firing with so many questions. Her heart just wanted answers so she could find her brother. Every time they made progress, more questions arose.

Ian took Paul. Was it because of her? Or did it have to do with the minerals thing? And who or what was CF?

The door opened again, and this time the ranger they'd spoken to stood there. "I'm sorry, but I'm going to have to ask you all to leave. The visitor center is closed and we need to start shutting down the office."

Nalani glanced at her phone. Past seven already? Out the window the sun shone bright as if it was the middle of the afternoon. Her stomach rumbled to remind her that she needed to feed herself. "Can we get some food on our way back to the office?"

Davin tried to hide his amusement at her body's protest by pinching his lips. Guess there was no hiding that lovely pronouncement.

"Can we at least stop and get some food on our way back to the office?" she asked.

"I know a quick take-out place. Fish and chips sound good?" Taylor slid her tablet into her backpack. "They have halibut, rock fish, or salmon, the three local catches."

"Sounds great to me. I'm not picky about which kind." She still wasn't used to all of the fresh seafood options.

Chicago offered cuisines from around the world, but she always tried to eat local when she traveled.

"I'll call ahead." Taylor pulled out her phone. "We can walk over there to pick it up to take back to the office before they close. It's only a block north of here."

They left through the back door of the visitor's center. The same door Paul had been taken through.

Nalani scanned the area. There were signs teaching people about the fjords and Resurrection Bay. When they left the courtyard behind the visitor center she saw the first ramp that went down to the docks.

She stopped and Taylor almost ran into her. "Are there cameras on the dock? They might have taken him by boat since he hasn't shown up on public cameras for two days."

Taylor sighed. "I thought the same thing. All of these cameras belong to the businesses along the docks. So far none of them were willing to let us look."

"Can't we get a warrant? There is proof that a man was taken." It took most of her composure to not shriek at the whole situation.

"There is only a video of Paul leaving with Ian." Davin scrubbed his face. "Without knowing what exactly happened, it's only conjecture that he was taken. No judge will approve a warrant."

"We need to do something." She grabbed hold of Davin's hand. "I can't just sit and eat when I feel like we're so close to finding him."

He looked down at their hands. She realized what she had done and went to release his when he gripped her hand gently, yet securely in his. "I know that it sounds like wasting time, but we need to keep our strength. After we eat we can ask the businesses again if they'll let us see their footage now that we know more."

She wasn't sure if it was his nearness, him holding her hand, or the hope that his words gave her, but she felt herself agreeing with him without a fight. This agent that she had pegged as a by the books, set in his ways man, was showing her just how deep he really was.

"We should get going." Taylor's words startled her.

Davin let her hand go. She immediately missed his warmth and strength.

"I will go tomorrow morning, first thing, to talk with those on the docks and see what video footage we can find." Davin put his hand on her back.

He guided her across the street to a small, cheery building with several outdoor tables and chairs. The smells coming from within made her stomach flip and grumble again.

The three ate in silence in the break room above the office space. Nalani crumpled up the wrapper and barely controlled her sigh of contentment. "That was quite possibly some of the best fish I've ever had."

Taylor gave her a half smile. "What's not to love about deep fried fresh fish? That close to the docks, you know it's never been frozen."

Nalani tried to stop the yawn, but with a full stomach and having only slept maybe an hour on her flight up here, the exhaustion was winning.

"You can stay here tonight." Davin threw his wrapper away. "Taylor can show you where to sleep."

"What about you?" she said through another yawn.

"I'll sleep out here on the couch when I get tired. It's a secure building and I'll double check all of the doors."

She wanted to push through and keep looking for Paul, but Davin's words from earlier didn't only apply to food. She needed to at least try and sleep if she wanted to be of any use in finding Paul tomorrow.

She scooted her chair back. "Wake me up to go to the docks?"

A flicker of something flashed in his eyes before he returned to his neutral expression, but she was too tired to figure out what it meant.

He reached his hand out to hers and pulled her to stand in front of him. It was probably the brain fatigue, but she could have sworn that his Adams apple bobbed, and his eyes slipped to her lips.

"I'll see you in the morning." The softness of his voice had all kinds of flutters rolling with the fish in her stomach.

She needed sleep so her brain could fight off her emotions again. "Good night."

Nalani stepped past him, toward Taylor, who waited for her in the hallway. She walked as fast as she could without looking like she was running away from him.

When she got to the hallway, she looked back over her shoulder. Could she have been wrong about him? Too bad she was the one not staying this time. She would have loved to uncover the mystery of Special Agent Davin Schulz.

Nalani rolled over in the surprisingly soft bed and flipped her phone up to check the time.

She blinked at the screen. How was it after nine in the morning?

She had slept for over twelve hours. That couldn't be possible.

Davin had said he was going to the docks early. Why hadn't he woken her?

She threw off the covers and went to rush from the room when her reflection in the mirror stopped her. Maybe a stop at the bathroom was necessary first. Her hair stuck up in different directions and she should probably have on actual clothes, not just a tank top and shorts before demanding to know what happened.

A few minutes later, feeling more human and less of a mess, Nalani set out on her mission to find Davin and demand to know why he went without her.

The smell of fresh coffee pulled her toward the kitchen. Taylor sat at the small table sipping from a mug and reading something on her tablet.

"Morning. Hope you slept well." She raised her mug. "There's more if you'd like some."

Nalani held on to her anger. Taylor wasn't the one who went to the docks. No, Davin was the one that deserved her fire, and she would save it for him.

"Is Davin back yet?" She sat down in the other chair at the table with a delicious smelling cup of coffee and picked an apple out of the bowl of fruit.

"He said that he'll be back for lunch and he's bringing barbeque as a peace offering."

"He wouldn't need to bring a peace offering if he'd woken me up like I asked."

"He tried." Taylor looked over her mug, an impassive expression on her face. "So did I."

Nalani's anger cooled a bit. "Can you tell me if he at least found anything yet?"

Taylor shrugged one shoulder. "He only texted that he needed to wait until a captain got back."

"That's not very helpful." Nalani crossed her arms and slouched in her seat. She probably looked like the angsty teen she was when she went to Rock of Hope Camp, but she was an adult now, so she would wait.

"Maybe this will help." Taylor pulled a chair over to her desk and woke up her laptop. "When Paul first disappeared, we pulled his finances to see if he'd left us a clue as to where he was hiding or taken. Everything looked normal." She opened up a window and spun the computer to face Nalani. "I sent up an alert that would tell me if something happened to one of his accounts."

Nalani squinted at the screen. "Paul or someone else, deposited fifteen thousand dollars into his account. I thought you said everything looked normal and yet this money deposited into his account the day he was taken. I don't understand."

"That's just it. It wasn't there when I checked the first time."

"So what? There was a glitch in the system?" Where was Taylor going with this line of questioning? Paul would never do something for that kind of money.

"I think they figured out who Paul was when they took him and are trying to make it look like he's dirty."

"Paul would never do that." This was bad. All the evidence Paul collected against these people would be tainted and his reputation would take a hit that his career might never recover from. Nalani winced. "I hate to give points to bad guys, but that is clever."

Taylor cracked her fingers and began typing, "Maybe, but I'm going to use this to find them. They don't know who they're up against."

Nalani hoped she was right.

# Chapter 8

The cool air crept past the collar on his fleece jacket as Davin sipped from his coffee cup. Nalani would be upset when she woke up.

The fishing charters usually set sail at six in the morning. He had tried waking her up, but a fog horn probably wouldn't have done the trick.

He was just thankful she found sleep. He, on the other hand, hadn't slept more than an hour or two.

Gray clouds rolled off of the mountains and into the harbor. It was probably going to rain again. He wouldn't want to live anywhere but the northern most temperate rainforest though.

Davin pulled his rain jacket out of his backpack and slipped it over his fleece. His hood was only in place a moment before the cold water splashed down around him.

He could wait inside the wildlife tour cruise place, but he preferred the salty fresh air surrounding the docks.

The door opened behind him. "Agent Schulz?" Sam, a tour guide with the company, stood inside out of the weather. "I have that footage for you now."

He checked his watch. He had waited an hour, but at least one of the businesses was willing to work with them.

"Thank you." Davin stepped inside. Droplets dripped off his coat and onto the rug. He shrugged out of his jacket and hung it on the hook next to the front counter.

Sam, in the typical navy polo and khaki pants uniform motioned for him to follow her through the door. She led him into a small office holding only two cushioned chairs, a few filing cabinets and a wooden desk. She clicked a few keys and gestured for him to take a seat.

"I was told to watch over you until you were done." She fidgeted from one foot to another.

"Thank you for letting me see the footage." He looked at the time stamp and moved the toggle to the time they last saw Paul at the visitor center.

Two men about the right builds walked down the plank to the docks. They turned left and went off the screen.

"Do you have another camera that shows the rest of the dock?"

"Possibly. May I?" She pointed to the computer.

Davin moved out of the way. In a few seconds she had a different camera from the other end of the building facing the docks up and running. It was focused on the walkway behind the building. Davin ran it back to the right time stamp.

Ian appeared in frame keeping his face away from the storefronts and the cameras, but Paul made sure to seek out the camera.

"Message received," Davin whispered.

Paul had to be trying to give them as much clear evidence as possible, giving Davin leads to follow. Which meant Paul wanted to be found.

The two men got onto the third boat before slipping out of the camera's view.

Davin squinted to read the slip number. "Do you know who rents that slip?"

Sam shook her head. "It's not one of ours. I can't see the name or numbers on the boat from this camera, but the one next to it is one of the fishing charters next door. The captain might be able to help you more."

"Great. Can I take this footage with me?" Davin prayed that God would let them have this one.

Sam winced. "I'm sorry. Mr. Whittle said that I could show you, but without a warrant, you wouldn't be able to take it with you."

Davin knew it was a long shot, but at least the owner had let him look at it. "Thank you for your time and help."

Sam sighed. "I hope you find him alive."

Davin prayed again as he stepped from one shop to the next along the docks. It was getting closer to mid-morning and the half-day charter passengers would soon start to show up for their trips.

*God, you're going to have to show up here. This is our only hope at finding Paul.*

Inside the next shop there were large pictures hanging on the wall boasting of past hauls. The place had fishing rods and nets mounted on the walls for decoration. It was rugged yet clean.

He rang the bell on the counter, its ring raking on his tired nerves. He rubbed his eyes and drew in a breath. Where were the employees manning the front desk? His hand hovered over the bell when a man with a white beard and crow's feet around his eyes stepped around the corner.

"I'm so sorry. My niece's son was sick this morning so I'm here by myself. I was in the back prepping the buckets. Never mind." The guy's flustered speech gave way to a professional tone. "Thank you for your patience. How may I help you?"

"Agent Davin Schulz, FBI." He showed the man his badge and ID. The business owner scrunched his nose and leaned close before putting on reading glasses. "FBI, well that's a first for my humble shop. What can I do for you?"

Davin slipped his wallet back in his pocket. "I was wondering if you were the one whose boat is in dock B slip 4?"

"Why are you asking about my boat?" The man squared his shoulders and Davin felt the wall starting to go up.

He needed to be careful if he wanted more answers.

"A man has been taken against his will and the last sighting we have was of him getting onto the boat next to yours. I was hoping you could tell me something about it or even who captains it."

The man relaxed and leaned against the counter. "Jackie could probably tell you about it."

"Your niece?"

The old man barked a laugh. "No, Jackie's my grandson. Although I wouldn't call him Jackie. Only his Pops calls him that." The man winked. "He is pulling into the harbor now. Go on down and tell him Pops sent you."

"What can I call the captain?"

"He prefers his given name nowadays. Captain John is my best charter captain and that has nothing to do with him being my blood." The old man turned to greet more visitors who had walked through the door.

*The Salty Lady* drifted back into the slip. The two crew members tied the ropes and expertly placed the fenders to prevent the boat from hitting the dock.

The man closest to Davin wore orange bib waders, a Henley shirt underneath, and peered at him with suspicion. "You are going to have to see Pops up at the store to get a boarding pass. We won't be taking passengers until noon."

"I'm not going on a trip out. Pops said I needed to talk with Captain John."

The man grunted and turned back to his work. A group of fifteen people disembarked followed by the other crew member who hauled a cart up the ramp full of the morning's catch.

The rain had dropped off to a thick mist, but the clouds still hid the tall mountains surrounding the bay. A man in his late twenties in rubber waders and a long sleeved shirt approached.

"You must be Agent Schulz. Pops radioed that you needed to talk with me. You're going to have to come aboard if you want to though. I have another group and only thirty minutes to get the ship ready." He ducked into the cabin without checking if Davin followed.

Davin scrambled aboard and followed John to the bridge. He was gathering supplies and paperwork then took off to the back of the boat.

John glanced over his shoulder. "What is it that you want to know?"

"Do you know who owns the boat in the slip next to yours? Or where they might have gone?"

John straightened, frowning. "Landon usually only takes people out on overnight tours. He left three days ago and hasn't been back."

"Do you know how I could get ahold of Landon? What touring company does he belong to?"

John shook his head, "He was trying to branch out on his own. He only has a website for people to book a tour. He does some of the more obscure places like Rugged Island, Fort McGilvray or ferrying kayakers to Aialik Glacier."

"Do you remember seeing who got on his boat when it was here last?"

Someone from behind Davin spoke up, "I saw two dudes get on board. The one was talking on his phone in Russian."

The crewman he first talked with was washing down the table in the middle of the deck as he spoke.

Someone talking in Russian on the phone must have been Ian. "You wouldn't know what he said by any chance?"

It was a long shot, but it was worth an ask anyway.

The guy lifted his chin. "My mom is from the motherland, but my Russian is a bit rusty. He said something about picking up sweet bread and going to the bunker. Or something like that."

John bunched his brows. "Did he say picking up sweet bread or at sweet bread?"

Davin wasn't sure what he was getting at, but he held his questions inside.

The crewman stroked his beard. "He said picking up at sweet bread, but that doesn't make any sense. That's why I said picking up sweet bread."

John shook his head. "Sweet bread isn't a thing. It's a place." John turned to Davin. "When the Russians controlled this area, they used to call Hive Island *Sweet Bread Island*."

So three days ago, Ian had been talking about making a pick up at Hive Island and then going to a bunker. Davin turned to the other crew member. "Do you remember anything else?"

"No, sorry man. He went into the cabin and the rest of his conversation was cut off."

"What about the other man with him?" Davin pulled Paul's photo up on his phone. "Did he look like this?"

"Yeah. That's him."

"Did this man say or do anything?"

The seaman pulled his eyebrows together and crossed his arms. "Come to think of it, he didn't say anything. He just stared at our boat like he was looking at us, but not really seeing any of us."

Davin's lips ticked. Paul wanted others to see his face, but didn't want to get caught trying to make contact.

Smart man.

Davin prayed that those instincts kept him alive long enough for them to find him.

Nalani paced the conference room. Taylor was working her computer magic and had let Nalani use the conference room to do some research.

Every phone call she had made in the last hour was a dead-end. She was no closer to figuring out who her father was than she had been when she woke up this morning. But it was better than being annoyed at Davin.

She wanted to bang her head against the wall, but decided that pacing to release her energy was better.

"Okay," she said aloud to herself. "Let's review what I've got. Mom had a summertime crush on Nick. When she tries to tell him about me, Gramps told her to go away. She's threatened to stay away from the family and she goes into hiding until I'm born."

Nalani stopped pacing and felt her throat tighten. Her mother really had loved her even if she had been young and alone at the time.

Her mother could have given her up for adoption, but instead she kept her even if it hadn't been for long. Giving her up wasn't her mother's choice, but one that had been forced upon her family.

Nalani's heart both expanded with love and crushed into a thousand pieces. Her bunkmate at camp, Rylie, said that those who believe in Jesus go to Heaven. Did her mom believe? She would have to ask her great-aunt about that.

Nalani took a cleansing breath and continued her pacing, thinking aloud. "Few months after I'm born, Mom and her brother are killed. Probably by Gramps, but we're not sure since it was ruled an accident."

She paused in mid-step and rushed over to the door. Sticking her head out she called over to Taylor, "You wouldn't happen to have any connections at the SPD to get me the file on my mother's accident, would you?"

Taylor gave her a slight grin. "I might have a favor or two I could cash in. Give me a few minutes to set this up to run while I get you that report."

Nalani made her way to stand behind Taylor. The screen in front of her started to flicker as the bar below moved slowly across the screen. She was running some kind of scan. "What are you looking for?"

"I've been trying to follow the money. We might just get a break and figure out who has Paul." She looked up at Nalani. "I'm hoping it'll be either a clue as to how Spartak is operating or maybe some more answers for you. Until then let's see if we can't get those files for you."

Taylor took out her phone and called her contact, "Peters, it's Ertz." Nalani could hear a soft chuckle but couldn't make out the words that came next. "No, I'm not calling for that date, I need to cash in a favor."

Nalani wandered over to Davin's desk. His spicy after-shave tickled her nose as she sat in his chair. There weren't any personal pictures on his desk. In fact, there wasn't much on his desk at all.

The plastic bin in the corner held a stack of papers and there was a raised platform with wireless keyboard and mouse all set up for his laptop.

The setup was not unlike how she liked to keep her desk. Her mess was usually contained to the digital idea boards on the cloud or to a white board she kept in her apartment. Growing up in the foster care system, she never had much in the way of personal belongings. Even the thought of clutter stressed her out.

Why did he keep his things sparse?

Taylor's words about a date made Nalani's heart want to scream out a battle cry. When was the last time she went on a date? Freshman year of college? That "date" if it could even be called that, had been a disaster.

These days she didn't date. In her not-so-vast experience no one wanted her and all her baggage. Her job which she loved, let her travel the world. Which meant little time for a relationship at home.

Being alone had never bugged her before.

Why was it bothering her now?

As she leaned back in the chair, she knew the answer. Davin's handsome face, broad shoulders, and trim waist filled her mind.

She barely resisted the contented sigh that bubbled up. When she first met him, all she wanted to do was tell him to go away. Until the bullets started flying. In that moment he had gone from pushy FBI special agent to a pushy protector who was as motivated to find her brother as she was.

Somewhere along the line her foolish heart started to win. She'd not only let him protect her, but she found herself watching the door waiting for him to return.

She crossed her arms on his desk and laid her head down. Wasn't this where Paul and his mom would tell her to ask God for guidance? That He would help her make sense of this whole situation or something like that?

She tried, but He never seemed to answer her prayers. Radio silence. So what would be the point?

"I got those files for you." Taylor's words broke her out of her internal pity party. "Peters said there wasn't much since it was deemed an accident."

Nalani didn't dare hope. There was a limit as to how many hits a person should have to take in such a short amount of time. "Thanks."

Nalani's phone pinged with the email from Taylor. She looked over at the special agent. The woman was smart, but her eyes held a haunted expression when she thought no one was looking. Something drove her to be Special Agent Taylor Ertz. Maybe one day, after they found Paul, Nalani could ask her to tell her story.

As a journalist, she always sought the truth.

*"Jesus is the Truth. Seek him, Nalani, and you will find true peace."* Her foster mom told her those words the first week she was with them. At the time she had been so angry with the world and searching for something to make her feel wanted. Seen.

Was she still searching?

"Ertz, do you think I'll ever find out who my father is?"

Taylor rolled away from her computer. "I don't know, but after watching you work all morning I believe that if any one can figure it out, it'll be you."

Taylor's words pushed the doubts away. She'd find all the family she'd have left. Including her father. And Paul.

Davin burst through the back door. "I think I know where Paul is."

# Chapter 9

Davin put the lunch on Taylor's desk and shucked the rain jacket off, shaking some of the water droplets across the desk. He wanted to get back to the office as soon as possible to make a plan and talk out his theory, but he figured neither woman had had lunch yet.

Nalani refused to open her food. She was probably furious that he hadn't taken her with him. Sleep was what she needed. He'd have to deal with her angst later. They needed to make a game plan to get their agent back.

She looked up at him and caught him staring at her. "Just tell me where Paul is and that he's still alive."

Davin pulled his sandwich out and sat at his desk next to her. "I was able to figure out the boat that Ian and Paul got onto. According to the witness, they were picking something up at Hive Island and then going to the bunker."

"Do you know what bunker?"

Davin didn't take a bite. Normally he would savor every piece of the sandwich, but the worry and hope radiating from Nalani made his hunger vanish.

He opened his laptop. "During World War II, Seward and the surrounding area along Resurrection Bay was fortified with forts, armories, and even battery guns to secure America's northernmost territory from being invaded." He pulled up a map of the different outposts in the area. "This is where Hive Island is. There are two forts that would have had bunkers in them." He drew a circle around the two with his finger. "Fort Bulkley on Rugged Island and Fort McGilvray at Cains Head. Both places are remote enough that only the most adventurous tourists, or locals for that matter, would be in the area."

He studied the map.

Nalani's soft words broke his concentration. "Where do you think he is?"

He had been playing that same question in his mind the whole way here. If Ian and Paul were going to Hive Island, Rugged Island was the next one in that chain of three in Resurrection Bay. Cains Head was part of a State Park surrounded by Kenai National Park and Chugach National Forest.

He rolled his chair toward Taylor. "Can you bring up those pictures you found on Paul's hard drive?"

The first picture of Aialik Bay and the surrounding area of Kenai National Park filled her screen. He clicked to the next one. A picture full of dark green trees with a road cutting through the far right edge came into view. Chugach

Forest. Cains Head didn't have any paved roads in or out of it. It was accessible by hiking in, so this was most likely not the forest beside Cains Head.

The last photo was of Rugged Island. There was a beach along Mary's Bay on the south side. This was where boats could get on the island safely when bringing tours to the island. The rest of the island had cliffs or jagged rocks surrounding it making it impossible to land anywhere else safely.

Paul must have left these three pictures because they have something to do with Spartak. "He's on Rugged Island."

"How do you know that?" Nalani's voice didn't hold doubt, only curiosity.

Davin stood. He clicked back to the first picture. "This is Aialik Bay inside Kenai National Park, not close to Cains Head. This one is of some part of Chugach National Forest. See this road? I'm not sure where in the forest this is located, but it's not Cains Head. The only way into and out of the State Park is to hike."

Understanding lit her eyes. "You think because Paul didn't tell us about Cains Head, he wouldn't be there."

Davin brought up the last picture. "This is Rugged Island and that" —he zoomed the picture closer— "is Fort Bulkley. At its height eighty men were stationed on the fort. They were the first line of defense for the port at Seward."

"Just because Paul didn't tell us about Cains Head, doesn't mean that they didn't take him there," she argued.

"True, but it's more probable that he's in a place that Paul has already connected to the group." Davin was sure that they would find Paul on Rugged Island.

Landing unnoticed and getting him back would be a whole different thing. He was going to need resources, which meant calling Anchorage and Special Agent in Charge Hollands.

"How are we going to get on that island?" Nalani had moved closer. Her familiar coconut scent pushed some of his unrest down.

Davin turned toward Taylor. "I'm calling Hollands to send some agents, then the Coast Guard since it's their territory. Can you contact Deputy Chief Levell? We're going to need their assistance."

"There's only one way to get onto that island." Nalani stepped in front of him. "How will you do that without being noticed?" Their faces were only inches apart. Her soft intake of breath and parted lips told him that she felt the connection between them as well.

He swallowed to push down the attraction, but his husky voice betrayed him. "We will find a way. We're trained for this kind of thing." He took her hand, unable to stop the action as if it was the most natural thing to do. "I need you to stay here. Where it's safe."

The tenderness and concern in her eyes turned to fire. "I'm going with you."

He shook his head with each of her punctuated words. "I can't allow a civilian to raid a potential terrorist compound. It is against protocol and for good reason." He sighed. "I wouldn't be able to forgive myself if something happened to you."

The fire of defiance turned to a smoldering ember. "At least leave me a radio so that I can hear what is going on."

Davin expected more of a fight from her, but he had an extraction to plan. "I'll post one of the Seward Police Officers with you. Several of them have military backgrounds and are more than capable of keeping you safe."

Her jaw clenched, but no argument came flying at him. "That sounds reasonable."

Was she going to attempt her own rescue of Paul?

Did she know something he didn't?

Davin tilted his head and studied her. The wheels inside that pretty head were turning. He would have to warn the officer not to let her out of his sight. A civilian getting kidnapped by Spartak was the last thing they needed.

Who was he kidding? If she was of no value to them, they wouldn't take her.

She would be dead.

The thought sent a chill down his spine. "Promise me that you'll stay with the officer? I need to know that you're safe."

Her eyes widened slightly. She wrapped her arms around her middle. He didn't like putting fear back into her features, but if it kept her safe, he would every time.

She dipped her head. "I promise."

Two hours later with the cold water spraying his face, Davin stared at the approaching set of islands. Nalani had surprised him when she gave him a hug before he left the office.

"Please come back," she'd whispered.

As if she needed him.

Wanted him back.

Officer Peters from the Seward Police Department had shown up to stand guard while he was gone. The man served two tours overseas with the Marines. Davin was confident in his ability to keep Nalani safe. Peters had texted to say they were upstairs and all was calm.

Davin silenced his phone now and shoved it into his pocket. If he wanted to get back to Nalani safely, this mission needed his full focus.

As they approached Fox Island, the radio on the bridge came to life. Davin snatched it up, earning him a glare from the ship's captain. He knew he was breaking maritime protocol, but he was in charge of the rescue.

Davin had flipped the radio to the secure channel before they left, keeping their communications away from other seafaring vehicles. "Mustang, this is Legend. Give me a status report."

The Mustang was a 110 foot Patrol Boat for the US Coast Guard that docked in Seward and patrolled the waters of Resurrection Bay and parts of the Gulf of Alaska. If they found these men on a boat, having the Coast Guard close by with all of the proper equipment and the authority to board a ship would give them an advantage.

"Legend, we are positioned on standby." The patrol boat was hidden in one of Fox Island's coves. They would be in a position to help immediately if needed. "Do not engage a boat without our presence. Over."

Davin resisted the urge to roll his eyes. He had been spending too much time with Nalani. Her spunk was beginning to wear off on him. Something he didn't seem to mind. "Copy."

Davin gave a nod to the captain who powered the boat toward Hive Island.

*Lord keep us safe.*

Nalani lowered herself onto the lounge chair on the balcony. Alaska was supposed to be the place of the midnight sun, but this late in the summer darkness was creeping back into the nights. The clouds from earlier were sticking around at least for now blocking out what little light the stars and moon would have offered.

What she wouldn't give to be there when they raided the bunker.

She turned to Officer Peters. "You wouldn't happen to have heard anything yet?"

The tall man with sandy blonde hair and hazel eyes gave her a half grin. "They've gone radio silent, which means they're getting ready to make landfall." He patted the device on his hip. "You sure you don't want to hold on to this?"

She shook her head. "I wouldn't be able to understand most of what they're saying. Just promise to keep me updated."

"For what it's worth," Peters shrugged, "Agent Schulz is one of the best according to Ertz."

Taylor's phone call to get the files on her mother's car accident flashed in Nalani's mind. She grinned. "So, you and Ertz..." she left the statement hanging.

Peters' cheeks pinked and he rubbed the back of his neck. "A guy can always try, but she's too married to her job."

Nalani inwardly grimaced. Those were the words her last date said about her. Nalani had always used her job as a shield to keep people away so that she wasn't hurt too much when they left.

Since Davin burst into her life with guns blazing, she felt the need for that wall starting to crumble. The reality of what he was doing pricked her eyes with tears. If something happened to Davin and they still hadn't found Paul, then she would lose two men who she cared about.

Swallowing back the bile that rose in her throat, she faced the biting wind, letting it clear her mind. Her body slumped with the next exhale. For the first time since she arrived at the VanKirk house, she didn't want to be alone anymore.

"Peters, do you believe in God?" Nalani continued to stare out toward the bay.

Peters leaned against the door frame. He laid his hand on the gun holstered at his side. "I do."

When he didn't elaborate, Nalani looked him in the eyes. "Does He actually care about everyone? Even the man who took Paul?" *Even me.*

"No." A smile broke out on his face. "He doesn't just care about them. He loves each of us. Even you, Nalani."

How did he know about her doubts?

A board creaked in the stairwell before she could ask him more questions.

"Go to the bunkroom and lock the door," Peters commanded and for once she didn't argue.

The police officer unholstered his gun. He kept himself between Nalani and the stairs all of the way to the hall that led to the rooms.

He turned toward her. Before he could say anything, two shadows emerged from the darkened stairs, silently creeping towards them.

Her mouth opened to scream a warning. Crackling broke the silence and Peters dropped to one knee.

He looked up at her with pain searing his face. "Run!"

Goon one stepped behind Peters and pointed his gun at the back of his head. "Do as you are told or he dies." The thick accent made her blood turn to ice. She would remember the voice that haunted her most recent nightmares.

She lifted her face to the man that had broken into Paul's house.

"Come with me. And I'll release your brother." Goon number two stepped closer to her. The light from the lamp casted an eerie glow across the man's scar. "A fair trade."

Nalani sucked in a breath. "Ian."

A devious grin hitched up one side of his face. "I see you are smarter than you look. Come with me and I won't kill the officer. You wouldn't want his blood on your hands."

He cocked his head. "Or maybe you are more like your father, no?"

He knew who her father was? How was that even possible?

Nalani's head was spinning with possibilities.

She dared a glance at Officer Peters. He didn't move, but he was taking in everything around them. Calculating. Trying to figure out a way to save both of them.

It had only been a few days, but the people of this town had already started to breach her walls. She wanted to stay. She cared about this place. She wouldn't let an innocent man be hurt for her.

Ian raised his hand as to signal his friend.

"Wait." Nalani took a step forward. "Don't hurt him. He has nothing to do with this."

Ian sneered, "Pathetic American with the bleeding heart."

Ian squeezed her arm and she let out a whimper. He dragged her towards the stairs.

She stole a glance at Peters. "Tell Davin I'm sorry."

Ian shoved her towards the stairs. Nalani tried not to stumble down the stairs as the two stomped behind her.

"Now, get me the package your brother left you." What was Ian talking about? There was no way she was going to hand over evidence against him.

The office was in shadows, but she saw the puzzle box sitting on Davin's desk. It was the only piece of evidence they had left out before leaving.

Ian followed her line of sight. "Get it." The cold hard barrel of his gun pushed into her back.

Her hands shook as she handed the box to Ian. He snatched it from her and cursed, or at least she assumed he cursed, since the word was in Russian. "What is this?"

"That is what you want. The package from Paul's bag." Ian roared and smashed the box onto the ground. It bounced and rolled away but stayed shut.

Nalani bit her lips to keep the grin from over taking her face.

"You could have just asked me to open it." Oh, how she wished she could control her sarcasm better.

Ian's shoulders rose and fell with deep breaths. He clenched his fists and his nostrils flared. "Grab her, Gregor." The next instant, the large man had snaked his strong arm around her waist and a gun was pressed to her side.

"I would watch your tongue." Ian bent to pick up the box. "This had better be what we want, or you will watch your brother die before we send you to work off your deception."

Nalani swallowed. That threat sounded ominous, but hopefully by now the team had Paul safely aboard their ship. Peters would call for help as soon as he could move again. She was sure of it.

And maybe, just maybe they'd be able to find her before she disappeared to some modern day gulag.

She tilted her chin up. "You have what you want. Now release my brother."

Ian sneered. "You are too much like your mother to be trusted." He gave Gregor a command in Russian and her hands were jerked behind her. She peered over her shoulder to watch the brute zip tie her wrists together.

"We first verify the package. Then we talk about your brother." Nalani figured that they wouldn't release Paul but she had to try.

*God, please let Davin find him and give me an escape.*

Nalani tried to keep her feet under her as the big man propelled her out the door.

An explosion lit up the night sky.

Both men turned away from her.

Nalani took off down the alleyway. If she could just make it to the restaurant at the end of the block, she'd be able to find help. Running with her hands behind her back made her pace slower. She also needed to be careful because if she fell there was nothing stopping her face from smacking into the pavement.

Twenty more yards.

Ten.

A scream ripped from her. Gregor pulled her by her hair back towards Ian. Her whole scalp felt like it was set on fire. She stumbled and tried to get her feet under herself again to alleviate the pain. He threw her down in front of Ian. Her shoulder broke her fall and pain radiated down her arm and across her neck. She moaned, not willing to give them any more satisfaction at her suffering.

Ian chuckled, but nothing about his laugh spoke of humor. "You stupid woman. Did you really think you could get away?"

The world tipped upside down as she was thrown over Gregor's shoulder. She started to kick and squirm.

"You can either stop or we make you stop." Gregor's deep voice tore through her bringing enough fear to make her still.

They threw her in the trunk of a car. Rough fabric pressed against her skin. Her shoulder throbbed in time with her heartbeat and she felt blood trickle across her palms from where the ties cut into her wrists.

A tear slipped down her cheek.

If God could hear just one prayer of hers, she hoped it had been tonight's.

As much as the darkness wanted to crowd in around her, she refused to believe she was alone.

*Davin will come for me.*

She felt the truth of that thought settle into her. She would do what she could to stay alive knowing that God have given her someone so she wouldn't have to be alone anymore.

But would he find her in time?

# Chapter 10

Davin settled his helmet and NVGs on his head. Strapping his assault rifle across his chest, he let the familiar weight of the gear calm him and focus the energy buzzing along his nerve endings.

He closed his eyes and prayed for each of the people in their group. Stg. Barreck from the SPD was an army ranger who rescued his fair share of people during his service. Stevens, Yost, Reist, and Kyle had been sent from Anchorage. The only agents that SAC Hollins would spare. Ertz and himself. A solid group that he trusted. But God would be the only one to protect them from unseen enemies tonight.

Nalani's face flashed in his mind. He said another prayer for her.

The explosion set off by Ertz and Kyle from across Mary's Bay rocked their boat.

They waited as he scanned the inlet. There was no one visible. He gave the signal and hopped from the boat to shore.

The wet sand and stones cushioned his steps as he took the few strides into the tall trees.

As they made their way through the forest, Davin was forced to use the compass on his watch. The canopy of the trees blocked most of the view of the mountain. This coverage would keep them concealed until the tree line broke.

The proposed entrance being used was only a few yards from the thick forest where only a sparse set of trees dared to grow. It was the most exposed they would be. He only prayed that the explosion drew enough of the guards from that spot they could get in without much of a fight.

Taylor and Kyle were waiting for them at the edge of the trees. The clouds had shifted, and the full moon skittered across the mountainside, making the NVGs not necessary yet. It also left them unprotected if they tried to make a run for it.

"There is one guard by the bunker entrance," Taylor whispered in her coms. Davin made a signal for Stevens and Yost to go around and subdue the guard.

"Cover me," Davin whispered to Reist.

Davin pressed his hand into the rough bark. The broken pieces of rock from the mountain's peak made being silent a challenge.

It was a short distance from here to the next tree. Davin resisted the urge to push himself faster. He didn't want to make his presence known.

He made his way toward the guard.

He picked up a cold rock and weighed it in his hand. He said a prayer that the distraction would work. When he saw the two agents behind one of the guards, he threw the stone as hard as he could in the opposite direction.

The guards looked towards the clattering rocks. Agent Stevens subdued the first guard and Agent Yost secured him with zip ties. Davin moved in behind the second guard at the same time. He snaked his arm around the man's neck until he felt the guard go limp. Yost came over to secure Davin's target too.

Davin pulled his elbow back and motioned with his forearm to tell the rest of the team to move forward. Each member appeared, gun at the ready, scanning the trees for any more guards.

Davin kept his gun trained on the hatch while Stevens opened it slowly.

After a beat, Davin stuck his head over the edge as cold musty air hit his face. There was a ladder that descended twenty feet or more illuminated by a dim light bulb dangling on a wire in the space below.

Taylor was the last to climb down and left the hatch open to aid in their escape. The space was wide enough for two men to pass each other. The stone walls arched overhead, but Davin could barely stand up without hitting his head.

The tap on his shoulder from Stg. Barreck told him that everyone was ready.

They made their way down the tunnel. They came to the first hall off the main. Davin held up two fingers and pointed down the offshoot. Stevens and Yost would take that route and report back.

Creeping further down there were two doors on opposite sides and one straight ahead. Davin peered into the small window of the door on the left. There was one guard in front of a table full of computer screens. The wall behind him looked to be full of tactical gear. He signaled to Ertz. One guard.

After giving him a small nod, she burst into the room shouting at the man in Russian. There was a thwack followed by the sound of a body thudding against the floor.

"All clear." Ertz's voice whispered across the coms. Kyle entered and turned to face the door as Ertz went to work on the computers.

Davin, Barreck, and Reist moved to the next door. Davin pointed at Reist, then at the door at the end. The man covered the last distance soundlessly and peered through the door.

"A set of stairs. Clear." Reist said. Davin signed for Reist to keep watch then told Barreck to cover him.

They could explore those stairs in a moment. Right now, they had one more room to search before venturing deeper into the depths of the bunker.

Davin peered in the window of the last door. Given all of his training, nothing could have prepared him for what he saw inside.

A single bulb under a shade hung from the center of the room casting a yellow haze over everything making it hard to see into the corners of the room.

Paul sat under the light head drooped to his chest, dried blood on his shirt. His legs and arms were secured to the chair.

With a few more signals to Barreck, the two-man team slipped into the room clearing each darkened corner before Davin knelt beside Paul.

"Paul. Can you hear me?" He tapped his friend on the face. "We're getting you out of here."

Paul moaned but did not open his good eye.

Barreck helped Davin cut the restraints and pull Paul to a standing position.

Davin tapped his coms. "We have the package. Meet back at the extraction point."

Exploration of the bunker would have to wait. They needed to get Paul out of here.

Flanked by Reist and joined by Stevens and Yost at the end of the hall, Davin and Barreck carried the semi-conscious agent to the bottom of the ladder.

Paul groaned when Davin shifted him to his back. Ertz appeared with Kyle. She nodded once.

They found Paul and she made a copy of the computer's hard drive. Now they just had to make it back down the mountain without getting caught.

Barreck went first and Davin followed.

As the group crashed into the woods, Davin heard angry shouts behind them. They needed to get off this island before they were all dead.

Tree branches slapped at his face and roots reached up to trip him. Every faltered step cost him precious moments, which allowed the Spartak agents to gain ground.

Davin's lungs burned. His legs shook under the extra weight of his friend. A bullet slammed into a tree beside him. He needed to keep moving.

Barreck sidled up next to him. He lowered Paul to the ground and the two looped their arms around Paul's waist. The trio stumbled through the last part of the thick forest.

They were the last to board the waiting boat. The captain piloted the boat back into the Bay, speeding towards the Mustang and Fox Island. The gunfire had ceased once the boat was safely away.

Davin laid Paul on the couch in the cabin of the boat.

"Call for medivac to Fox Island," Davin shouted over his shoulder to the captain.

He looked over Paul's injuries in the brighter lights of the cabin. His right eye was completely swollen shut and he had multiple abrasions across his face.

It seemed that Ian or one of his men used Paul's head for a punching bag.

"Hold on, Paul. Help is on the way.'

Paul grabbed his arm with surprising strength. He whispered something that Davin couldn't make out.

Davin leaned closer. "Find Nalani. Before Ian." Paul went into a coughing fit.

"Captain. We need..." All words vanished as Davin took in Ertz's shocked expression.

She handed him the radio without a word. "Go for Schulz."

"Special Agent Schulz. I'm sorry...taser...Nalani..." The communication cut in and out.

Davin's heart slammed into his chest. He must have misheard. "Repeat that Peters."

"They took Nalani."

The relief of finding Paul alive shattered into a thousand pieces.

How could this happen? She was supposed to be safe.

When Paul disappeared, Davin had felt a sense of duty to find him. Now that Nalani was missing, it was deeper than that. It was personal.

He wasn't sure when it happened, but the woman made him see that there could be more to life than the job. He needed to find her. Nothing would stand in his way.

They hadn't killed her. Yet.

Either they hadn't figured out she gave them an empty box or they were plotting a way to make her body disappear. Nalani blew at a strand of hair that dangled in front of her face. Her hands were still bound behind her, which caused her shoulder to continue to throb.

Gregor had thrown her into the small bedroom inside one of those vintage RVs. She sat on the thin mattress with her knees pulled to her. The vehicle rocked as they continued down the road.

Where were they taking her? Deep into the wilds of Alaska? Great, she wasn't even sure if Davin would find her if she ended up there. She'd probably waste away to nothing, dying a slow torturous death or getting eaten by a bear.

*I am with you.*

She lifted her tear stained face. Who spoke those words? No, she hadn't heard them. More like they appeared in her mind.

Rylie's advice filled her mind. *"Sometimes God speaks to us. All we have to do is listen."*

Could it be that God really was there? And that He cared about her?

Nalani leaned her head back against the wall and closed her eyes, "God, I'm not sure that was you, but if you're listening, please send someone to save me. I'd like to learn more about You. Rylie said You love everyone and You would hold me in Your hands."

Her aunt's words from earlier crashed into her. *"She made me promise to keep you a secret. To keep you safe."* Every foster home she had been in played like a reel in her mind. She had been moved once a year, sometimes more, but with each home she had been safe. Cared for even when she was not easy to love, which sadly was not the case for some children in the system.

"You really were with me. Protecting me." She shuttered out a breath, "Thank you."

The vehicle slowed down. Nalani stood up and leaned against the wall to brace herself. There was not much room between the bed and the walls. If she fell over though, it would be difficult for her to get back up with her hands bound in the tight space.

A door slammed and Nalani tensed for whatever was coming her way. When the door to the small room slid away, Ian stood there with a sneer.

"Where are we going on this glamping trip?" The sarcasm wasn't going to save her, but it did make her feel better.

She lifted her chin making herself as tall as possible. Ian chuckled. The sound turned her blood as cold as the artic waters of the Alaskan Gulf.

"You will do what you're told or your brother dies."

Her heart sank. Davin hadn't found Paul. Or worse, he died trying. A sob threatened to choke her. Until she knew that fear was true, she would hold out hope that they were both alive. She had already talked to God about it.

Ian sneered. "That pathetic excuse for an FBI agent won't find you or your brother."

She sucked in a quick breath. What if Paul wasn't on Rugged Island? What if they were being set up? "I want to see him. Where is Paul?"

Ian pulled out the puzzle box. "When I know the plans are secure, I will send for your brother."

He took a step toward her invading her space. She resisted the urge to take a step backwards, biting down on her back teeth.

"He had better be alive when you bring him." She put as much bravado into her voice as she could.

Ian slid one side of his mouth up. "That is up to you."

The blow came out of nowhere and made her stumble backwards. The air rushed out of her lungs as she stared up at his smug face. Ian turned on his heels. The door rattled as it slid back into place. Nalani took a few deep breaths until her lungs felt like they would work normally. The man had a strong upper cut. She should have known better than to provoke someone without a soul.

She rolled to her side and let the sobs flow from her. Davin couldn't be dead. God wouldn't be so cruel, would He? Every good foster home though was stripped from her, so maybe He wasn't as all loving as Lydia made him out to be.

*I am with you.* She let those words repeat through her until sleep won out.

The click of the outside door had her sitting up quickly. Gregor's frame took up most of the small space before her. "Stand." She stood. See, she could follow directions. "Turn."

Everything in her told her not to turn her back towards an enemy, but she wasn't sure what would set these guys off and get Paul killed. With her back to him, she squeezed her eyes shut, bracing for whatever torture was sure to follow. The clink of a chain sounded right before she felt the cold ruff metal on her ankle. She followed the chain as Gregor secured it to the wall. When he walked back to her, every muscle in her tightened, but relief flooded her as her arms fell to her side followed by a throbbing pain in her shoulder.

Gregor tossed a tray on the bed. "Eat."

Either the man didn't know much English or he was truly a man of few words. She needed to find out as much as she could.

"Where are we going?" Stretching out her arms she tried to get the flow of blood and her nerve endings working again.

"Do what you're told and you just might live."

Nalani opened her mouth to ask another question, but Gregor had already closed the door. The camper swayed as he left.

Nalani sank onto the bed. She looked at the bread and cup of broth with what looked like rice floating in it. She would survive this. She had just found her mother's family and Davin. For once in her life she didn't want this chapter to be over.

She would keep her strength and her wits about her. If Davin and Paul didn't come for her, she would have to look for an opportunity to run. This wouldn't be the first tight spot she'd gotten herself into.

Nalani drank the soup quickly while scanning the room. Now that she had her hands free, she needed to see what she could find to help her.

The chain on her leg clanked as she moved. She'd find an escape route then figure out how to get out of the chain.

She crawled across the bed toward the small window. There was a blind drawn, but it was nailed shut. She pulled at the side, ripping a small piece of the blind away. The window had privacy tinting on it, meaning she could see out, but anyone passing would most likely not see her.

There was a thick forest that faced the back of the trailer. Chances of someone walking close enough was slim.

She ran her fingers around the frame of the window. There was no latch. She could try to kick it out, but she'd look for another option first.

Nalani rolled off the bed. The clamp on her ankle rubbed at her skin. She sucked in a breath. She'd need to be more careful when moving around until she could get the blasted thing off.

As she crouched on the floor, she stared at the bed. One of her fellow journalists was telling her about their camper. She had said there was storage in all kinds of places including under the bed. Nalani ducked lower. There were no drawers visible. Hope started to deflate in her chest.

She ran her fingers under the mattress like she had done with the window. There was a break in the frame between the board the mattress laid on and the bottom half. She hoisted the board and mattress up.

Inside the bottom frame was a storage area. With nothing in it but an old blanket. She ripped the blanket out and threw it on the floor. Nothing. No tools. No broken wood. No help.

Nalani growled. She squeezed the edge of the mattress she still held. Just this one time she needed God's help. Before she let the board go to slam shut on yet another dead end, a small hole in the back of the space caught her eye.

Stretching as far as she could without letting go of the board, Nalani leaned close to the opening. She stuck two fingers into the space and pulled. The whole bottom of the compartment moved only a few inches. The wood had warped making the tight cut almost impossible to move.

Nalani squinted into the darkness. What was down there? She tugged on the wood again making little progress. The outside door opened and shut. Nalani lowered the bed back into place as quietly and quickly as she could. She'd bide her time and get that space open. She could do this. She had to.

# Chapter 11

Davin paced the stony shore of Fox Island. The stones made his legs work harder for each step, but the strain matched the torment inside. "What do you mean she's gone?" He fired the question at Deputy Chief Levell. The Deputy Chief had met them at Fox Island and was the one that called in the medivac.

How could she be gone? How could he let this happen? She trusted him to get Paul back and to keep her safe. He had failed. The overheard conversation after he got his orders to start the Seward Field Office rang through his head.

*"I can't believe Schulz got the placement."*

*"You know it's only because of his father. When he fails, and he will, they'll put someone better suited there."*

It was the anthem he heard most of his life. One that he worked hard to prove wrong, but it turns out they were right. He did fail and he failed miserably. He didn't deserve this post. Did SAC Hollands give this to him as a favor to his father?

"Sir, we will do everything in our power to find her," Levell reassured him. "Officer Peters is collecting evidence outside your office now."

"Does he know which direction they took her?" The endless possibilities of where she could be pelted his mind.

"Peters said that the back door was intact. The two assailants came in from a window in the front of the building. They found the trap door into the office." Levell paused. Davin's gut dropped even further to his knees. "He said that they tased him then held him at gunpoint and forced her to go with them. He found the footage outside your back door. Nalani tried to get away, but the man with Ian threw her in the trunk of a waiting car."

Facing Taylor, he barked an order, "Go with the Mustang back to shore. Help SPD collect evidence and figure out which way they went."

If Ian took evidence before they were about to crack the encryption code, they might not be able to stop whatever plan Spartak was going to enact.

"Peters said that it looked like Ian was carrying some kind of box with him in the video," Lavell continued.

Davin reached for the Deputy Chief's phone. "I want to talk with Peters."

There was a shuffling on the phone, then a gruff voice. "Sir."

"Tell me exactly what you saw on the video."

Peters winced out a breath. A faint apology came through the line. The man was probably getting checked out by medics. "There was a flash off screen and Nalani took the distraction to make a run for it. She only got a few paces before Gregor got to her. She was kicking and pounding until Ian leaned close and said something. Gregor then threw her in the trunk of a dark sedan."

Davin's pace slowed as the police officer retold the story. "Any chance we got a license plate?"

"Negative, Sir." Peters' words were muffled as he talked away from the receiver. "But there is a report of an abandoned vehicle that matches."

That was fast, but Davin wouldn't celebrate until he had Nalani back with him. "Send me the address. I'll meet you there." Davin handed Levell his phone back.

"Special Agent Schulz?" The director of the resort ran to him pointing across the bay. He could now hear the faint thwomp of helicopter blades.

Davin went back aboard the Legend to prepare Paul for transport. He needed to tell Paul that Nalani was missing. He didn't even know she was in Alaska let alone captured by the very group he just escaped from.

Davin reached Paul's side. "Help me secure him for transport." He spoke with Reist and Levell. They stretched and secured straps so that Paul wouldn't shift on the litter while in flight. Paul only grunted when they placed the strap across his head.

Davin's phone buzzed. Ertz's number flashed on the screen. "Did you land already?"

"Hardly, Sir. I was able to access our interior cameras via the secure network on the Mustang." Davin wanted to yell at her to spit it out. Time was not on their side. "Ian told her to give him the package her brother left him or else he'd kill Paul. Nalani gave him the puzzle box, but nothing else."

Nalani gave Ian exactly nothing. When Ian figured that out... Davin shivered. "We need to find her now." He hung up.

"Find who now?" Paul's raspy voice made Davin turn.

Davin knelt beside the litter they had strapped Paul to and braced himself to drop a bombshell on his friend. "When you didn't respond to her messages, your sister, Nalani, came looking for you."

Paul's hand fisted, but said nothing.

"She's been helping us find you." Davin continued.

"You let a civilian help with an investigation?" Paul seethed through gritted teeth.

The accusation stung. "I was protecting her. They had shot at us, left a note threatening her life, and attempted a kidnapping in town the only time I left her out of my sight. So, yes, I let her help us because she was safest next to me." Davin ran a hand through his hair. "I don't know if you know this, but she is an excellent investigator. She could get secrets from the president if given the opportunity."

Paul's eyes narrowed and one side of his mouth ticked up. "Break her heart and I'll break your nose."

Davin pulled back. What? Sure, the woman had impressed him and she was beautiful beyond her golden flecked eyes that saw everything and that silky hair his fingers itched to run through.

She believed in him and made him want to be the best version of himself. Did he really like her in a romantic way? He was fooling himself if he could forget the feel of her skin or the way his mind was calling out to God for her safety.

Somewhere along the line he let their attraction slip past his focus of deserving this post. All the more reason to deny his feelings.

"I don't..."

"Save the argument for yourself. Where is my sister?" Paul reached for the straps holding him down.

"Woah, there. You are going to take the helicopter to Anchorage. I will get Nalani back."

Davin's phone vibrated. The sound of the helicopter made talking difficult. Thankfully, this was a text from Officer Peters. The abandoned car was the one that Nalani had been taken in and it was at the Seward Airport.

"Change of plans." Davin raised his voice so Levell could hear him over the noise. "I'll catch a ride with Paul and have them drop me at the Seward Airport. Your guys found the car they took Nalani in."

Fifteen minuets later they were lifting off the shore of Fox Island. The pilot, Luca, looked over at Davin with a grin.

"Haven't flown a rescue mission since I left the Swiss Royal Air Force." He pulled back on the toggle and turned them towards Seward. "Elmendorf usually flies the rescues. But when the FBI called for help, I couldn't exactly say no."

SAC Hollands had a deep reach. One that Davin was grateful for right now.

Davin looked back at Paul. "I'm not going to ask what happened," Luca spoke into the headset. "Are you sure you don't want to go with him to Anchorage?"

Visions of Nalani being put into the trunk of a car flashed in his mind. "No. I have a more pressing situation to handle."

Luca cut him a glance, but didn't ask any more questions.

The harbor came into view and Luca lifted them a bit higher. Davin could see the Mustang pulling into port with the sailors and agents pouring from its deck. Hopefully by the time he got to the airport Ertz would be back at the office to secure everything there.

"Here we are," Luca announced. "Looks like you're chasing trouble tonight."

Blue and red lights flashed in the predawn twilight. They had a large spotlight on a dark sedan and one officer sealed off the area.

Luca set the bird down gracefully. "I hope you catch whoever you're chasing, mate."

"Get him to Anchorage." Davin took one last look at his fellow agent. "SAC Hollands should be waiting for you at the hospital," he said before hanging the headset on the hook and ducking out the door.

Davin jogged from the landing pad to the alley between the darkened buildings boasting helicopter tours and dog sledding on glaciers. The road connecting all of the small buildings along the runway ran along the main road heading into Seward and dead ended in thick forest on one end. The car surrounded by police activity was parked on the opposite side of the road from the buildings.

"Peters," Davin called as he approached. "How do we know this is the car they drove?"

Peters reached a gloved hand into the trunk after lowering the camera around his neck. He held up Nalani's cell phone. Davin's breath hitched. Without her phone they wouldn't be able to track her.

Peters shifted on his feet. "It's not your fault, Peters," Davin tried to reassure the officer.

Peters dropped the phone into the evidence bag and sealed it. The thud of the phone hitting the bottom of the bag made Davin's mouth go dry.

*God, we could use a bit of help here.*

"Agent Schulz. You'll want to see this." The other officer, Hicks, called from further down the road.

Davin rushed over, still careful not to disturb too much of the area. Officer Hicks was squatted next to a set of tracks in the mud by the side of the road.

"Looks like they were in a larger vehicle." Hicks pointed to where they pulled away. "They were pulling a trailer behind them." Now that Hicks had said it, Davin saw the second set of tracks following the same course.

"That idiot and his brute of a friend left almost an hour ago." Davin swirled around as a man in jeans and flannel stomped off the deck of the nearest building. "They went north in a hurry."

Davin had so many questions, but he needed to know if Nalani was still with him. "Did you see a woman with them?"

The man stuck his hands in his pockets and rocked back on his heels. "Didn't see a woman, but the large guy was coming out of the camper when I came out to tell them to keep it down." They could have stashed Nalani in the camper.

Peters took the man's statement and Davin walked away to check in with Ertz. They needed to figure out where these guys were going. Seward was at the southernmost point of this stretch of highway. Most of Alaska was north of where they stood.

He had been so close to finding her.

"We're coming for you Nalani." Davin whispered into the wind. He wouldn't give up until she was in his arms. Safe. Where he hoped she might want to stay.

The measly meal did not do much for the rolling in her stomach. She had lost track of time since they started back on the road again.

"God, me again. I know I'm probably not high on your priority list, but Lydia says You take care of all our needs. I need my strength and wits about me. Could you get me out of this camper?" Nalani sighed. She wasn't sure how this praying thing worked. Lydia made it look like she was having a conversation with a friend. Nalani could use a friend right now.

The drone of the tires begged for her to rest. What she needed was a way to open that compartment under the bed. She had a feeling that it would lead to a way out of here.

Time marched on, but with no watch, phone and blinds covering the only window, Nalani had no way of telling what time of day it was. She had tried sleeping, but closing her eyes allowed her subconscious to torture her with situations of what ifs. Her eyelids kept pulling down despite her efforts at avoiding the terrors.

The slowing down of the vehicle had her jerking awake again saving her from one nightmare, but landing her in another. There were noises scrapping from under her, then the outside door opened. The camper listed to one side before righting again a moment later. The door closed with a thwap that made her limbs start to shake.

Where were they? Was this where they would get rid of her? She needed a weapon, anything to defend herself.

The click of the lock on the sliding door stilled her frantic search. Gregor stood in the doorway. She wasn't sure if it was the lack of sleep or situation, but the look on his face looked less lethal than it had last night.

He bent to her ankle and unlocked the bracelet allowing the chain to fall to the ground in an eerie clatter. "You run, I shoot."

Nalani swallowed and nodded once. She had no doubts of the man's threat, but was still thankful for the reprieve of no bounds. Gregor shoved her toward the door.

Her hand slammed against the metal frame sending pain through her injured shoulder. She sent the man a glare which made him hitch a half grin at her. Just when she thought he had a heart, he smiled at her pain. Running was now out of the question, at least with Gregor standing so close to her.

With another shove Nalani stumbled down the short hall toward the small kitchen and living area. Ian sat on the tiny couch with the closed puzzle box beside him.

"Do not draw attention to us or innocent people may die," Ian seethed and looked out the window.

Next to them was a tent beside a campfire. A small child was blowing bubbles with his mother.

Nalani could not put this child in danger. She'd do what Ian said for now.

Gregor dropped his arm around her and pulled her out of the camper.

What on earth was happening? She stumbled down the two steps, but somehow he kept his grip on her. His hot breath skimmed across her neck, "You need to do what he says and make sure no one else gets hurt."

Gone was the broken English fortified with a Russian accent, in its place was a twang she was familiar with from her years at Alabama University. Nalani tried to look at him.

"Eyes forward." Gregor pushed them towards the bath-house. "I need you to get a message to Agent Schulz. Spartak is changing hands and Ian is making his move to be next in line once the old man dies."

Was he talking about Alexei? What exactly did Ian have planned?

Who was Gregor? Could Nalani trust him? Was he the one that God was sending to help her escape? He certainly knew who Davin was and he did only tase Officer Peters instead of killing him. That was something right? Nalani didn't know what to believe.

Before Nalani could choose which question to ask first, Gregor removed his arm and pushed her toward the bathhouse door. "Do your business. No running. Or else." Nalani looked into Gregor's eyes. There was no trace of an ally there. Only a darkened void.

Had she imagined the secret message he just gave her. She wasn't a spy or a special agent. But she was a reporter and she knew that there was a story behind Gregor. One that she wanted to uncover.

On the way back to the camper she tried to dig out the truth. "Who are you?" she whispered.

Gregor only responded with a grunt and small shove to keep her walking ahead of him. She wasn't sure how, but the henchman's true alliances appeared to be closer to hers. She only needed to work that to her advantage and escape.

When they got back to the camper, Gregor sat down in a chair outside. "Ian wants to talk with you inside." The man refused to look at her.

The family next to them was nowhere to be seen. At least they weren't in immediate harm. Nalani's stomach began to roil again.

Nalani ascended the stairs and stepped inside. A shiver wracked her body. "God, could use that help right about now," she whispered.

"No one is going to save you." Ian sat in the same spot, but the box was now open, "Did you think that you could trick me?"

Ian stood in a flash. He fisted her pony tail in his hands and yanked her to sit where he had just been. Thousands of sharp needles sent fire down her scalp. She swallowed the scream.

He smiled at her. "You may be more like me, your real brother, than I first thought."

"I'll never be anything like you." She refused to break eye contact with him even though her head swam with the implication of Ian somehow being her flesh and blood.

Ian then started to laugh, throwing his head back. "The same blood runs through our veins. His blood." Ian spat. "He'll never see it coming because he'll be too shocked that the only woman he's ever actually loved is alive again."

Each of Ian's words were slamming into her with the force of a heavyweight boxer's blows. The puzzle pieces were clicking together.

"Alexei Volkov is my father?" She stared at Ian's smug face.

Ian was the one threatening her to stop looking for her family. "Why didn't you want me to know that?"

*Smack*. Nalani toppled over, but managed to stay on the couch. Her check stung and her shoulder throbbed, but as long as she had breath she had a chance of getting out of this.

Ian let out a string of Russian which she could only guess at its harsh meaning. He bent again so that his face was only inches from her own. "Your *mother*," he sneered, "was the reason that Alexei is ruining our family's legacy. She filled his head with ideas of contentment and letting go of his anger toward those who took everything from our family."

Spittle flew from his mouth, but Nalani's heart filled with hope. If her mother could be such a force of good then maybe she could be like her.

Her lips slowly rose. "She sounds like someone I want to be when I grow up."

Ian roared before his fist connected with her side and she felt the air rush out of her. She coughed and tried to get her lungs to work again.

Standing just inside the door, Ian faced her one more time, "Then it is time for you to fulfil her legacy and die."

Nalani curled on her side allowing the tears to come. Her father was Alexei Volkov, Russian businessman who was known for his shrewd business deals. According to the article she had found about him, he was well respected in the business world, but he also gave off this persona of a man one should not cross in a deal.

She closed her eyes and pulled up the pictures she had found back when they thought he was the one in charge of Spartak. He was an older version of Ian with grey along his temples, but the custom cut suit made him look refined.

Gregor slid into the seat across from her. The scowl on his face did not bode well for him being willing to help her.

He leaned closer and lowered his voice, "You need to do what Ian says. Don't try to run away. If Schulz is as good as his reputation, then he'll find us and he'll be able to stop Ian."

She searched his face looking for signs of deceit. His hard jaw and drawn eyebrows made him look harsh. His eyes shown with light for a moment then a veil fell down over him. She didn't know how anyone could pull themselves out of reality and pretend to be the very evil that they fought against. Paul had to do that when he went under-cover.

"Did Paul know who you really are?" Nalani dared a question.

"No one does." His Russian accented voice made goose-flesh ripple across her body. Whether he was friend or foe, she wasn't sure, but he was the only one that she had right now.

# Chapter 12

Davin pushed the accelerator as fast as his driving skills allowed. Paul was being held overnight for severe dehydration and observation. He wanted to debrief his agent and get the encryption code for the SD card he left.

"Tell me you've finished scanning the download from the bunker." Davin dared a quick glance at Taylor who bent over her laptop in the front seat.

"I'm not superwoman. But I did finish tracing where the money in Paul's account came from." Taylor punched a few more keys. "I was able to trace the shell companies back to a Russian company roughly translated, 'Black Horse'. They seem like a company on the up and up." She pointed at the screen. "Says here that they supply copper to different companies that create motherboards or batteries for cars."

Davin gripped the wheel. They already knew that Spartak was from Russia. The group was somehow connected to a company that supplies copper wholesale.

Davin shook his head. What they needed to do now was find Nalani. He could work through the details about Spartak after she was safe. Ever since Paul's statement about Davin's denial of his feeling for Nalani, he would give up even this post if it meant that he could get to know her better.

Davin passed the slower moving car on a stretch of straight road. "What have you gotten so far from the bunker computer?" They needed some information that would tell them where Ian took Nalani.

"I'm searching the files." Taylor's fingers flew over the keys again. "We have file after file of video surveillance. I'll keep looking."

Normally he would have enjoyed the ride from Seward to Anchorage that twisted through the mountains and then skirted along the waters. The beauty centered him and helped clear his mind, but with Nalani out there with Ian, not even the wilds of Alaska could settle him. He needed to turn to the only one who could give him inner peace amongst the turmoil.

*God, keep our girl safe. I'd like to get to know her more. Give me peace right now and allow me to be the force you use to rescue her. Send an angel to look over her until she's free. Amen.*

Davin breathed out and felt the tension in his gut give way to the peace he knew was only coming from God.

They parked as close as they could to the entrance to the hospital. Taylor's scan of the bunker hard drive yielded nothing but video surveillance. Helpful for building a case against Ian, but not for finding Nalani.

Davin came into the small private hospital room. Paul laid on the bed with butterfly bandages on his forehead and an IV pumping fluids into him. His agent, his friend, was going to make it. A small knot in his chest eased.

"You here to bust me out of this place?" Paul tried to smile, but grimaced instead. "Did you find Nalani?"

The relief he felt earlier vanished in a single breath. "We need to know where Ian would take her. Or even why."

Paul took a deep breath. "When Ian took me to what he calls "the office" there was a picture of a woman on the desk. I had to do a double take because at first glance I thought it was Nalani." Paul swallowed hard. "I asked Ian who the woman was and red crept up his neck as a vein along his temple bulged from his anger. He slammed the picture down so no one could look at it anymore then responded, 'Someone my father refuses to forget.'"

This detail made Davin's heart stutter. Nalani's mother was somehow connected to Alexei Volkov?

Davin furrowed his eyebrows. "Joyce said that Nalani's father was named Nick."

Paul winced. "Ian's father is Alexei Nicoli Volkov."

A chill matching the bite of the arctic swept up his spine. "We need to find her. From Officer Peters' description, Ian and some other man were the ones who took her. If he was that upset over a picture of her mother, I don't want to think about how he feels about her."

A dark cloud settled over Paul's face. "Did you find out what was on the micro SD card? Ian was getting suspicious. I hadn't had time to break the encryption before I hid it for you."

"Not yet." Ertz spoke up from behind him. "We were able to connect Spartak to a Russian company supplying copper for wholesale."

Paul sat up in his bed.

"What is it Paul?" Davin barely controlled the bark in his voice.

"I overheard Ian talking about copper deposits on his family's land. I originally thought he meant in Russia, but what if this is about more than just rare metals?"

"Taylor, look into the Volkov family." Davin crossed his arms over his chest. "Focus on the late 1800s."

Taylor sat on the plastic covered chair in the corner. "What are you hoping to find, boss?"

"It's something Nalani said about Lysander taking back what they thought was rightfully Sparta's." Davin massaged his temples.

"You think that Spartak is trying to stake a claim on land here in Alaska?" Paul asked.

"With the push from our government to find rare earth metals on US soil, it is going to be like another gold rush," Davin admitted. "Whoever owns the land where they find it could live a comfortable life off of the mineral rights."

"The Critical Minerals Summit is in Fairbanks tomorrow. The who's who of scientists, environmentalists, engineers, and even lawmakers. Senator Schulz will be there giving a speech about finding minerals for America inside our borders." Paul looked at Davin.

"Do you think that Ian would hit the summit?" Davin stared at his agent. If there was a threat to the summit, then he needed to get SAC Hollands to mobilize a team to stop it.

Paul ran his hand through his dark hair. "I planted a bug in his office, but only got his side of the conversation. That's why I stole the card. It has all of Ian's plans on it."

Paul slouched back in bed. "It's what got me caught in the first place. Ian doesn't trust anyone and his right-hand man suspected me from day one."

"We'll get a full briefing once we have Nalani back." Davin gave Paul a long look. The man had been through the wringer, but he was more determined to take down Ian than anyone in this room.

"As soon as this bag finishes." Paul nodded toward the almost empty saline bag. "I'm out of here."

Davin stepped toward him. "You need to get better." He rested his hand on Paul's shoulder. "We will find Nalani."

Paul shrugged out from under Davin's hand. He threw the blanket back. "I'm coming with you."

Davin put both hands up. "Fine. As we wait for the refusal papers, let's start with all you do know about Ian's plans and where he might be headed right now."

Paul ran through what he was able to uncover about Ian's operations. "The bunker is used as some kind of packing facility. Ian keeps all of his shipping records at an underground shelter near Aialik Glacier."

"Is that why you gave us the picture of the fjords?" Davin started to pace. "Do you think Ian took Nalani there?"

Paul shook his head then winced. "I doubt it. Ian was focused on the summit. It starts tomorrow." He swung his legs over the edge of the bed. "I don't know what he has planned for Nalani, but it's nothing good."

Taylor's computer dinged and she sucked in a quick breath. "Boss, look at this."

He stood over her shoulder as the pictures on the screen came into focus. A curse formed on his lips, but he pushed it back down. "I need to make some calls. Figure out a plan. We need to be able to stop this before anyone else gets hurt."

A soft moan escaped her lips as Nalani sat up slowly. When this was over she would sleep for a day or maybe even a whole week. Every muscle in her back screamed at her, her legs felt stiff and heavy. It wasn't the ideal condition to be plotting a way to make a run for it. Although, with enough adrenaline, she wouldn't feel most of the aches and pains.

At least they had removed her chain while she attempted to sleep. She stumbled through the door and slammed into a hard wall.

"The princess finally wakes up," Ian sneered as he towered over her.

"If I'm a princess, what does that make you? The dragon keeping me in the tallest tower?" Ian's laugh sent a chill through her. Nalani wrapped her arms around herself but refused to cower.

"See we could have had great fun together growing up." Nalani squinted at him. This was not her definition of fun. She was focused too much on his face that the prick of the needle took her off guard.

"What did you just give me?" She waited for darkness to come over her or for her mind to start to lose its grip on reality, but her thoughts ran as fast as her heart. Nothing seemed to change.

"Just a little something to make sure you die when you are supposed to." Ian sat back at the small table checking something on his computer

She would somehow find Davin and he could take her to the hospital. Hopefully they could reverse whatever Ian put in her and she wasn't destined to die before she got the chance to explore whatever was happening between her and the special agent.

*Do what he says. Find Davin. Don't die.* Mantras helped her in the past to stay focused on the story she was chasing down, so now she'd use one to stay alive long enough to take down her half-brother.

Ian closed the computer with a dark smile. He opened up a cabinet and pulled out a bin. Setting it on the table with a thump, he turned to her. "You have two hours. There are a change of clothes and toiletries in the bag." He hitched his thumb in the direction of a navy blue bag on the floor by the door. "You are meeting your father. Make yourself look nice."

Nalani's hands shook as she gripped the leather straps of the small duffle.

Gregor tugged a baseball hat on his head and stepped up next to her.

"Follow me." He grumbled something in Russian which made Ian smirk. The exchange punctured a Texas-sized hole in her hope that he was here to help her. Maybe she read his gesture wrong. *Or he could just be trying to stay under the radar with Ian*, she half-heartedly persuaded herself.

Once outside she scanned the other sites looking for someone that could at least get a message to Davin. She would never put a child at risk so the family next to them was out, but a retired military guy who was probably armed would be a nice ally right now. The weight of Gregor's arm fell on her shoulders.

"Don't run right now." The 'Bama drawl was back in place which made her shoulders relax a fraction. "No matter what I tell you, keep walking toward the bathhouse, and you can't let on to Ian that you know. He will kill us both and throw us into the Chena River."

The tension snapped her shoulders back again. Nalani slowly nodded her head. She didn't know if her voice would work, but she had to find the strength to do this. To survive.

"Ian is putting a bomb at the Critical Minerals Summit. He's somehow using you as the trigger." Gregor lifted his free hand to wave at a couple as if this was a normal day.

"What does that mean?" she squeaked past the dryness in her throat.

"Ian will put a tracker in your purse. When the signal arrives at the targeted space, the bomb will detonate." They stopped at the door to the bath house. "Agent Schulz and his team will be there. You need to find them before you make it to wherever Ian is sending you."

"You make it sound so easy." She took a deep breath through her nose and asked the question most occupying her mind. "What did he give me?"

Gregor put both hands on her shoulders so that she faced him. "A high dose of Warfarin. I'm afraid if you don't get a Vitamin K treatment to counteract it in 48 hours, you'll bleed to death internally."

The blood fled from her brain so quickly that she felt herself tipping into unconsciousness.

"Woah." Gregor shook her shoulders gently. "You will be alright. Just try not to fall or injure yourself."

She tipped her head to the side letting her curiosity spur her. "Who are you?"

Gregor withdrew his hands from her shoulders and a hardness returned to his features as he fisted his hands and looked at the ground. "A ghost."

The words were barely audible and held the weight of the world in them. The journalist in her wanted to know his story, to help him get out of this brooding world he was trapped in.

She reached out her hand to touch him, but he took a step back, "Take your time." He nodded toward the door, "I'll be out here waiting."

Turning the water as hot as she could stand, she let the pounding spray wash away part of the last few days and the tears that streaked her cheeks. She opted to brace her hand on the cement wall to keep her upright instead of sliding to the cement floor and completely losing it for just a moment.

Even though Gregor told her to take her time, she knew that she needed to pull herself together and find a way to rewrite the ending that Ian had planned for her. If he thought she would go down without a fight, then he needed to learn a lesson from his older half sister. That thought sent a shiver down her spine.

She had always dreamed of the day she found her parents, her family, but now she wasn't so sure that the mystery was best left unsolved. Joyce's face flashed through her mind. She desperately wanted to survive this and hear more stories about her mother.

Alexei Volkov was her father. If Ian was any indication of what her father was like, she wasn't sure if she even wanted him to know she existed. But Ian's words gave her a bit of hope when he accused her mother of making Alexei want to be better. Ian saw it as a character flaw, but Nalani held on to the prospect that Lorelai's influence made at least part of her father into a good man.

Nalani pulled a white sundress with bright yellow sunflowers on it out of the bag. Below it a pair of under garments—she wasn't going to think of how they guessed her size correctly for those. Folded on the bottom of the stack was a pale yellow cropped sweater. Clearly they didn't get the memo that yellow was her least favorite color, but she couldn't complain about the change of clothes too much. She glanced at the dingy pile of her t-shirt and jeans. She may just tell Gregor to burn those for her.

As her fingers brushed across the bottom of the bag to pull the sweater out, she felt something hard under the lining. There was a small cut at the seam that she could barely fit two fingers through. When she made contact with the hard object she tugged it from its secret spot.

It was a burner flip phone with a note attached to it.

*'Don't take the necklace off. Text 309.76.667.33 to Schulz. Trash the note and phone.'*

Nalani stared at the note then looked back into the bag. There, tucked into the corner, was a silver sunflower necklace. Gregor may actually be the angel she had begged God to send.

With shaking hands she punched out a text and sent it to Schulz, thankful that she had a penchant to memorize things like phone numbers. She needed to send him something that he would know was from her since this wasn't her phone.

A smile crept up her lips as she hit send. Now all she had to do was stay alive. And not let Ian kill so many innocent people.

# Chapter 13

Davin rode up front in the first black SUV as they breezed through the gate to the private end of the Anchorage International airport. Most of the planes that used this runway were bush planes coming in from the far reaches of Alaska. Flying in several different planes would make it difficult to organize themselves, but if he rode with SAC Hollands, then they could at least make a plan and get everyone else on board after they landed.

When the first SUV pulled up next to a Bombardier Global private jet, Davin had to blink a few times. How did Hollands get such an expensive ride to Fairbanks? He knew that people's lives were at stake, but this was beyond his expectations.

Davin jogged up to his boss who stood at the bottom of the stairs to the craft, "Sir, I'm not complaining, but how did you secure this ride on such short notice?"

Hollands smacked him on the shoulder. "Alexei says to find his daughter." Davin stared at the jet. Hollands smirked, "Get on board and take a seat at the larger table. You're taking lead on this operation."

Hollands wasn't taking over? His confidence in him put the doubts to rest in his head. He earned this post and he would prove it to himself and the other agents.

Davin ascended the stairs and was greeted by a woman in a business suit. "Welcome aboard, Agent Schulz. Mr. Volkov thanks you for your thorough work. Would you like me to take your bag?"

"I'll keep it with me, thank you." Hefting the bag further up on his shoulder, Davin entered the cabin.

Three of the agents were already sitting in various white leather recliners. There were two facing each other around a small coffee table right inside the door. Behind that set were four large chairs around a table. Across the center aisle, were two more seats.

There was a wall behind that set of seats. Davin stuck his head through the opening. In this area, there was a couch along the one wall with a large screen TV and another recliner along the other. Alexei could conduct business up front and then relax towards the back.

It was possible that Ian would change his plans now that he no longer had the SD card. He was arrogant enough, though, that Davin doubted he wouldn't capitalize on the opportunity to take out the two people who stood in his way.

SAC Hollands joined Davin, Ertz, and Paul at the table.

"Something has been bothering me," Davin started. "Ian doesn't seem to be the man at the top. He's clearly the one planning this attack, but this one seems personal to him, not necessarily Spartak. So who is the man at the top? Do they know Ian is trying to take out his own father?"

Paul faced him. "Ian does take orders from someone across the ocean, but he never trusted me to be privy to those conversations. The bug in his office tipped me off about Ian dealing with 'his own problem'." Paul shifted in his seat. "I was unable to get to the bug before Gregor revealed me as a cop." Paul pinched his lips to the side. "I've never been able to figure out how he made me. There was something about him that seemed familiar, but I haven't been able to figure it out."

"We can have you sit with a sketch artist after this trip and see if we get a hit," SAC Hollands said.

"We've been unable to get a picture of his face off of any of the cameras." Davin shared his screen with the TV behind them. "We know that Ian and Gregor, his right-hand man, are here in the States. There hasn't been any chatter about any more operatives joining them."

Davin pulled the blueprints for University of Alaska Fairbanks up on the screen. "This is where Senator Schulz is set to give the keynote speech for the Critical Minerals Summit."

All four of their phones dinged with a message from the senator's head of security. *Senator refused to cancel or live stream his speech. His compromise was that he requested more security.*

This wasn't even close to being a good plan.

"Doesn't he get it?" Davin pounded the table.

"If the Senator wants to be live bait then we can use this to our advantage." Hollands' calm yet demanding voice pushed his frustration to the side. "Let's look over the maps and make a plan."

The short hop to Fairbanks gave them just enough time to forge a plan. They would complete another scan of the buildings for any unaccompanied bags or packages. Every bag entering through the door would be searched.

The blueprints for a bomb were among the encrypted files. There was no scale on the plans. So, it was hard to tell how big Ian would make the bomb.

Three armor-plated SUVs awaited them on the side of the runway when they came to a stop near one of the hangers.

"Alexei sent us a plane and a ride?" Davin spoke the thought aloud, unable to suppress his gratitude.

"No." Hollands nodded towards the vehicles and put his phone away. "These are from good old Uncle Sam and a certain senator that wants us to brief him on our plans to keep them all safe."

Davin snorted. "And if something goes wrong, it'll be all our fault." Hollands tilted his head and swept his keen eyes over his face.

He was clearly letting his past with his father shade his judgement. Davin stood tall and didn't back down from the hard stare.

"I put you in this position because I know what kind of agent you are, not because of him." Holland jerked his thumb towards the SUVs. "Get out of your own way and do your job."

Davin chewed on those words while they made their way through Fairbanks. Pulling up to a log cabin, the vehicles stopped.

A man appeared on the porch flanked by two secret service agents. Harrison Schulz wore his typical business suit, but his solid build was hard to mask under any jacket. Even though he had long been retired from the Marines, he still kept up with a rigorous fitness routine.

After making introductions with the head of security, Kirk and the other security agent, Hollands let Davin lay out the plan. "We will sweep the building for a bomb before you arrive. We'll also have Richards on over-watch in the rafters of the lecture hall." Davin swept his hand over a map of the lecture hall indicating where each agent would be placed.

"Since we found plans for a bomb we're going to focus on securing the building, but we'll take no chances." Davin continued with the briefing until every agent's assignment was fleshed out.

"I feel comfortable with this plan. Let's make it happen." Harrison Schulz rose to leave.

Davin's phone pinged with a message from a number he didn't recognize. He opened the messages app and sucked in a sharp breath.

"I just got a message from Nalani." Davin stood knocking over the chair he had been sitting in. "It's a series of numbers."

Paul came around to stare at the message. "How do you know it's from Nalani?"

Davin stared at the words again. *When you find me, I'll buy you a blueberry scone from the church and some Raven's coffee. -Your favorite journalist*

"It's her." Davin nodded. "This looks like an IP address. I need..."

"Go." Hollands cut him off. "I'll call Good Feather at the Fairbanks office and ask him to spare you a few agents to help track her down. Between the two of us, hopefully we'll catch Ian and bring Nalani home safe."

Paul took a step with Davin towards the door. "I'll go with you."

"No, Special Agent VanKirk." Hollands barked the order. "You have intimate knowledge of Ian and the Volkov family. And you are injured. You will be staying here. Special Agent Schulz will find your sister."

Paul's nostrils flared, but he didn't object to the direct order. "Bring her home."

Davin would do just that. Bring her back with him and somehow persuade her to stay so that they could explore the feelings he no longer wanted to deny.

First he needed to find her.

Alive.

Words were lost in the thickness of his throat. With a solid nod he made his promise to Paul.

"Davin." Senator Schulz's commanding voice stopped him halfway down the front steps. Davin turned to face his father. "I'm guessing from that exchange this woman means something to you."

Davin bit down on his back teeth to keep the hard retort about his father's lack of care. "I do," he managed to grit out.

"If anyone will be able to find her, I know you can. You've become a fine agent even if the director didn't listen to me when I requested you be transferred to Langley to be closer to your mother." He paused. "And me."

Davin blinked. His father requested that he would be transferred closer to D.C. so that he could be closer to him?

"SAC Hollands saw something in you that I got to witness today. I'm proud of the man you've become. Now go find your girl." Without waiting for a reply, his father disappeared back into the cabin.

What had just happened? His father was proud of him? This would be something he'd have to work through after he found Nalani.

Nalani walked with Gregor back to the camping site sans the phone, which she left on and threw into the trash can. Her hand itched to play with the necklace that was her life preserver right now. She only prayed that Davin didn't ignore her text since it wasn't from a number he recognized.

For someone who never prayed before, she had been doing plenty of it the last few days. Which, if she was honest with herself, was why she wasn't freaking out about the fact that she would have to somehow stop a bomb from going off and make it to the hospital to save her own life.

Sliding her eyes towards Gregor, she took in his profile. He was handsome when he wasn't brooding, which only happened when he knew Ian wouldn't be able to see him. What did he mean by being a ghost? Was he some kind of spy operating on American soil?

"Can you at least tell me your real name?" The question emerged before her brain could keep it in.

His jaw twitched and he stayed silent long enough that she didn't think he would answer. "Right now, people call me Gregor Petrov."

"So not John Smith." Gregor looked at her. A glint of humor was in his eye. As fast as it appeared, it was replaced by a void. "Will you ever be able to tell me your real name?"

Gregor stopped. "I hope so." He whispered so quietly that she strained to hear him.

"Give me the bag." The heavy Russian accent he switched back to grated against her frayed nerves. She much preferred the sweet Alabama draw.

She handed him the bag then followed him the rest of the way to the site in silence.

Ian sat waiting for them in a foldable chair as if he really were on vacation enjoying the Alaskan wilderness.

"A shower did you well." Ian stood and looked her over from head to toe which made her skin crawl. She'd need another shower after this was all over. "He will be distracted by both the sunflowers and you that he won't know what hit him."

"Why the sunflowers?" Of all the things she could have asked that question flew out first. She felt, though, that it was significant to her past.

Ian curled his lip, "Every year Father throws sunflowers over a bridge as some sick way of never forgetting the woman that ruined his life."

All the muscles in her body tensed. How dare he speak of her mother that way. Taking a deep breath through her flared nostrils she opened her mouth to argue with him, but Gregor shifted beside her. The movement helped her refocus her attention so she bit down on her molars shoving the angry words back down. Arguing with a psycho wouldn't do her any good.

Ian chuckled. The sound brought anything but humor with it. "Too bad you are dying. I would have had great pleasure tormenting you, *Sister*."

Opening the door, he pulled out a large leather purse with sunflowers across the bottom and the phrase *'Keep your face to the sun and you cannot see the shadow'* scrolled above them. The shadows is where she found herself currently, but the prayers were helping her not lose hope. At least not yet.

He shoved the bag in her hands. "I will be able to track where the bag goes, so do not try to ditch it in a dumpster or any other stupid idea you may try to come up with. If you vary from the path, I will set off the bomb."

Nalani wanted to pull the bag apart to find the tracker, but she gripped the bag tighter instead. "What about the innocent lives of the people in the lecture hall?"

"Senator Schulz is not as innocent as he makes everyone believe he is." Ian swatted her notion away as if it were an annoying mosquito. "The blast will only take out those on stage and those waiting in the green room. People in the audience should survive." Everyone but her because one blast or cut and she'd bleed out before they could get her to the hospital. "Remember the closer you are to the stage the better chance you won't feel a thing before you die."

This man needed to be in a psychiatric hospital. Who thought like that?

The FBI would be there. But have they found the bomb?

"What if I refuse to do this?" Not her best argument, but it was all she had.

"Then your brother dies." Ian shrugged as if killing anyone was a normal bargaining chip. "He's not your blood anyway."

"He is more of a brother than you will ever be. If he dies, my new life goal will be to make sure you pay." Her words shocked her. She wasn't usually the vindictive type, but Ian didn't even flinch at her venom.

As he stepped closer there was a gleam in his eye. "Too bad you are going to die today."

Nalani bit down on her tongue to keep her next smart retort from surfacing. She would not die today. Hiking the bag up on her shoulder, she started walking away. She should have kept the phone.

Ian's hard hand grabbed her. "Not so fast. The party doesn't start until later. For now you wait inside with me."

Gregor stepped forward this time and handed her a piece of paper. There was a map on the top highlighting a walking path across the university campus. "I will take you here." He tapped the map where a building was circled. "You will walk the rest of the way."

Nalani sneered. She could pretend that he was despicable too. "Don't want to show your face on camera?"

He gave her a hard stare. The man was good. She would say another prayer for him, too.

Davin had to have gotten her message. She'd have to come up with a way to get rid of the tracker.

Gregor opened the door and pushed her up the steps. Nalani took a step as her vision swam. She stumbled slightly then closed her eyes. Blinking them a few times helped clear the haze from her sight. The hospital is where she needed to be going. How long did she have before the concoction killed her?

Gregor dragged her towards the bedroom. He tossed her on the bed and bent past her.

Nalani started to shake her head. "No. Don't put that back on me. Please."

Gregor grunted and clamped the cold metal bracket on her ankle. The weight of it sank the bit of hope she had of trying to make it out of this tiny prison on wheels.

Gregor placed both hands on either side of her. "No running." She desperately wanted to see a light in his eyes. The dark pools showed nothing but hatred.

When he stood up, something small lay on the bed. Nalani placed her hand over the small metal key.

She waited until the outside door clicked shut before moving. Her fingers shook as she bent towards the clasp. Metal scratched against metal and she froze. What if Ian was still in the camper?

She crawled over the window ripping another piece of the blind away. Gregor dipped his head towards Ian and Ian revved the engine of a motorcycle as he pulled away. Nalani ducked her head and willed the tears to stay at bay.

She needed to act fast. Surely Gregor wouldn't stop her from running away. He gave her the key.

She jammed the key in the bracelet and turned it with a click. The metal clattered to the floor as the door slid open.

"We've got company." Gregor pushed past her and hoisted the bed up. He ripped the wooden plank that had stuck for her out like it was nothing. Below it was a storage area that looked like it led outside. "Announce yourself so they don't shoot."

Gregor sank down and pulled the bed on top of him.

Banging on the door made her jump. "FBI! Ian Volkov, come out with your hands up!"

# Chapter 14

Jarred Good Feather, Mylee Winters, and Jordan Burton, the three agents from Fairbanks, and Davin had taken their positions around the camper. The drawn curtain over the windows made it next to impossible to see into the camper. What Davin wouldn't give for a drone or infrared optics. They were going to have to do this the old fashioned way.

Jarred, who leaned against the tree next to him, nodded, which was the signal they were going to approach the camper. This was the part of the plan that was the most dangerous because it left them exposed. Davin told Jarred to take lead because it was his people's lives at stake and he hoped that Jarred would return the favor if ever in his territory.

Davin tapped his comms link and waited for the double beep in return. Winters and Burton were in position and waiting. They would be on the opposite side making sure Ian didn't slip out the back.

Good Feather covered the distance with hardly a sound as Davin trailed behind him. Each of them took the positions on either side of the door.

Jarred pounded the door, "FBI! Ian Volkov, come out slowly."

*Bang. Bang.* The bullets broke through the thin camper walls and sent Jarred stumbling backwards.

"Officer down." Davin said into his comms as he dragged Jarred behind the picnic table.

Good Feather moaned, "I'm fine. Gonna hurt for a few days. Thank God for Kevlar." Jarred pressed the comms button. "Winters circle around. Burton, cover the rear."

Jarred readjusted his position and winced. "Get this guy."

Davin turned towards the end of the table. "Ian, you are surrounded. Put down your weapon and come out."

The babbling of the small brook was the only thing that answered his command. Even the birds had gone silent among the chaos Ian created.

"You need to put down your weapons and come out. If we come in, it will..."

A heatwave tore through the air as the camper burst into flames. Davin shielded his eyes as he scanned the area for signs of life. Nalani could still be in there. He needed to get inside.

"Does anyone have eyes on the suspect?" Davin coughed as thick smoke closed in around them.

He got under Jarred's arm and helped him stand. "I can walk. Secure the area. I'll call this in." Jarred held his side as he limped away.

Mylee met him in the road with her weapon drawn. "No sign of him coming this way."

Two shouts rang out behind the trailer. Davin and Mylee took a wide berth around the flames only to catch a glimpse of Jordan sprinting into the woods.

Davin turned towards the camper. Was that a scream? "Winters, stick with Burton. I think someone is still inside." *Nalani could still be inside.*

Jarred came around the backside of the camper. "Looks like he crawled out of the storage area."

Davin waved his hand to silence the other agent. "Listen. Do you hear that?"

The roar of the flames strangled all the noise around them. There. "Help me! Davin!"

Davin was down on his hands and knees, sticking his head into the storage compartment. The stale smell of long forgotten air was mixed with the faint scent of burning synthetic fabrics.

The board above him scrapped, but stopped. A coughing fit sounded on the other side.

"Nalani?" Davin turned to get his feet under him as much as he could in the small space.

"Davin! Help! The fire is getting closer." The panic in Nalani's voice gave him focus. He pushed with all of his strength against the board. It moaned and started to bend when he burst through. The wood flew up, knocking Nalani to the ground.

Davin was inside the room, lifting the piece off of her. Relief flooded him.

He had found her.

Nalani was safe.

Free from the board, Nalani dove into his arms. "I knew you would find me."

The camper groaned as the door and wall of the bedroom were swallowed by the flames.

"We need to get out of here." Davin waved his arm toward the storage area. "Let's go."

Nalani crawled from the storage area and screamed. Had Ian circled back?

Davin rushed forward, smacking his head against the support bar. He rolled out of the opening in time to hear Good Feather say, "I'm Special Agent Good Feather. I'm here to help."

Davin took Nalani's hand and they ran away from the camper. He stopped them and pulled her into a hug.

"I thought I lost you," he whispered into her hair. She stuttered out a sob and clung to the back of his shirt.

Jarred had unhooked the hose from the camper and started to hose down the flames that licked up the sides. The water hissed and steamed as the flames started to die.

A gunshot echoed through the trees followed by a growl filled with pain.

Davin shoved Nalani to the ground and covered her with his body. He scanned the trees but saw no sign of Ian or the other agents.

"Officer down." Winter's voice crackled through the radio. Burton had been shot.

Davin slowly lifted himself off of Nalani. "Come with me. I've got to get you out of here."

She pulled her hand away from him. "Ian is going to plant a bomb at the summit."

Davin took a step towards her. "We know. There is a team headed that way to look for the bomb."

Relief slumped her shoulders and she swayed.

"Nalani. Let's sit down." Davin led her to the picnic table in the next site.

Sirens screamed closer as fire engines barreled toward them. Help was here even though Good Feather had most of the flames out. The men poured from the truck and took over the efforts to save the rest of camp.

Nalani swayed again and clutched her head. "Woah, there." Davin put his arm around her to steady her. "I need a medic," he shouted toward the company of firefighters.

A tall man in full turnout gear jogged towards them. "What seems to be the problem?"

"We need to f-find...b-bomb." Nalani's words slurred and her head fell back on his shoulder.

Davin took her face in his hands and gently lifted her to face him. There were red spots under her eyes and she blinked several times but did not focus on him.

Was this simply exhaustion or an adrenaline crash? Or had Ian done something to her?

"Excuse me, sir." A different firefighter carrying a dark duffle bag pushed Davin aside.

Davin paced the small camp site. He couldn't lose Nalani now. He had just found her and he hadn't been able to tell her how much he wished she would stay.

The two men lifted Nalani onto the picnic table and continued to examine her. They placed an oxygen mask over her face and she sat up. Davin strode toward her. She gave him a weak smile from behind the mask.

Jarred approached them, a dark expression on his face. "Burton was shot in the shoulder. He's on the way to the hospital with Winters. The man they chased got onto the back of a motorcycle being driven by Ian."

Davin put his hands on his hips. "I thought Ian was the one shooting at us."

Nalani shook her head and tried to pull the mask off. "You need to leave that on." The firefighter pushed the mask back into place. "You also need to go to the hospital. I don't like the spots under your eyes." The firefighter held Davin's gaze. Davin nodded his agreement. He'd make sure she was taken to be seen.

"Winters is sure the man driving the motorcycle was Ian." Jarred was typing something into his phone. "They turned right onto College Road before Winters lost track of them. They were headed towards the University of Alaska Fairbanks."

*Where the critical minerals summit was kicking off tonight.* Davin filled in the unsaid words.

Nalani pushed herself off the table and swiped off the mask. "Would you both listen to me?"

Davin faced Nalani and his heart dropped to the ground. He rushed to her side. He wove his fingers in hers and searched her face. What had Ian done to her?

Something warm slid across Nalani's lip and she licked at it without thinking. The taste of metal ran along her taste buds as her hand flew to her nose. Dark red dripped from her fingers when she pulled them away.

The firefighter, Stevens according to the name on the back of the jacket, ripped open some gauze and handed it to her. "Tilt your head forward and pinch the bridge of your nose."

She knew she had to get to the hospital, but she needed to tell them everything first so that they could save lives.

Nalani opened her mouth to speak but started to cough. Air. She needed to take a deep breath and try to stop this spasm.

Davin's large hand gently patted her shoulder. The gauze was saturated with blood and she couldn't tell if her nose had stopped or not. With one more deep breath, she straightened and let the tears roll. As his gaze roved over her face, his brows pinched together and his lips turned down.

"What did Ian do to you?" Davin asked with pain etched in his voice.

Nalani swiped at her nose only to feel more blood. Another gauze appeared in front of her and she took it. "I don't remember what Gregor said was in the syringe, but he told me to get to a hospital within forty eight hours to get Vitamin K."

Davin interrupted her. "Wait. Gregor helped you?"

"Yes. I don't know who he is, but he is the only reason that you are here. He was the one that gave me the burner and the tracking device." More tears stung her eyes. She needed to pull herself together so she could stop Ian.

Stevens shifted closer to her. "You said you needed to get Vitamin K within forty eight hours. When were you injected?"

Nalani swallowed. "This morning. Maybe an hour or two ago."

Stevens ripped off the blood pressure cuff and check the pulse oximeter. "We need to get her to the hospital. The other ambulance is on the way. You need to keep the oxygen on."

He pushed her hand holding the mask back toward her face.

"No." She made to stand, but wobbled right into Davin.

"I've got you. Let's sit and you can tell me whatever you need to." Davin lowered them both on the seat of the picnic table.

Nalani needed to clear her head, but her thoughts swam in and out. She had to tell him everything she had learned about Ian.

"Ian hates his father. He thinks he betrayed the family name by not fighting for the rights to the land they had once owned." She shuttered out a breath. "He said my mother ruined Alexei. She is the reason he stopped with the illegal dealings and is fighting to keep the land undisturbed."

Nalani continued to cough. Blood droplets sprayed across the ground.

Davin's eyes widened. "Where is that ambulance?" he shouted over his shoulder.

She wiped her hand across her mouth. "I'm okay for now." She exhaled to calm her lungs. The smoke still clung inside and made her lungs itch.

"He had planned to use me as the trigger to set off the bomb," Nalani continued. "He put some kind of tracker in the purse that would set it off when I got close enough to the stage."

She shut her eyes and leaned her head on Davin's shoulder. "Alexei is supposed to introduce Senator Schulz as the keynote speaker. I was supposed to approach Alexei when the Senator was walking on stage. I think he wanted to kill both of them."

She lifted her head slowly so the dizziness stayed at bay. "Is Senator Schulz your father?"

Davin's lips drew into a thin line. "He is. He also refuses to cancel the speech in person. I don't know if it is his confidence in his security team or pure stubbornness."

He clenched his jaw. She reached up and ran her fingers along his cheek. She felt him relax under her touch. "I prayed God would send someone to help me." Her eyes fell to his lips. His Adam's apple bobbled. "I'm glad He sent me you."

"Nalani." The husky whisper sent the butterflies in her stomach a flight. She wasn't sure if she had moved toward him, but their lips were only inches apart.

"Schulz." Agent Good Feather cleared his throat. "Sorry to interrupt."

Davin turned his head to face Good Feather, but kept her close to him. She raised the mask back to her face trying to inhale as much oxygen as she could praying that it would clear her lungs and head.

"Hollands checked in." Good Feather shifted and winced. "They found a device under the stage. The bomb squad was called in. They are delaying the start of the summit until everything is all clear."

Relief flooded her. They had stopped Ian. "Did you find Ian?" Her hoarse voice matched her fragile state.

A dark expression crossed the agent's face. "No he and his partner could be anywhere by now."

She shook her head careful not to send her into a dizzy spell. "He won't stop until Alexei and the Senator are dead. Now that he knows that I exist, I'm probably on that list too."

The cool air filled her nose. Her lungs still ached, but the coughing was better. She would never let Ian win.

"I won't let him get to you." Davin pulled her against his side. The move made her feel safe and wanted. Things that she hadn't really ever felt with anyone before.

Even with all of the oxygen flowing through her mask, she felt herself drifting. Had she lost that much blood? She had so much she wanted to tell Davin. They needed to catch Ian. He couldn't be left to hurt anyone else.

She fought against the weights that pulled her limbs down, making them impossible to move. She wanted to hold on to the feel of Davin's arms around her, but he was starting to slip away from her. Would he still be here when she woke up? For once in her life, she prayed that someone would choose her. Stay with her. Love her. And she wanted it to be Special Agent Davin Schulz.

Her eyes were drifting shut as the sound of a siren wailed in the distance. "Davin..."

# Chapter 15

The plastic seat creaked under Davin as he shifted to try and release the discomfort in his legs. The ride to the hospital had only taken twenty minutes. He had begged God to let her live.

When she lost consciousness, his heart fell to his knees. She couldn't be gone. He had just found her. He had so much he needed to tell her.

The slow rise and fall of her chest was the only thing that kept him from becoming an emotional mess. He had been trained in helping a victim deal with the stress of situations, but he never thought he'd be the one having to take the training to heart.

Davin scraped his hand over his face. He needed a shave, some coffee, and about ten hours of sleep. Sleep would have to wait, but he might be able to find something that passed for coffee around the hospital.

A cup appeared in front of his face. The strong nutty smell was enough to wake him up. He took the proffered cup from Paul's hands and took a long sip.

Paul worked his jaw and stared at the doors to the ER. Davin knew his expression bore much the same.

Davin let the dark brew dance across his taste buds. "Thanks. This hospital has good coffee."

Paul snorted. "The tar I found would have put you in the ER bed next to Nalani, so I asked a nurse where to get the good stuff." Paul took a long drink of his own cup.

Paul released a long breath as he sat in the chair next to Davin. "You doing okay?"

Davin looked at him from the corner of his eye. "I should be the one asking you that question. How many blows to the head did you take in the past week? Not to mention that Nalani is your sister, which you failed to mention."

Paul's grin hitched up on one side. "She can be tough on the outside, but all she really wants is to find where she belongs."

Davin let the fact that Paul didn't answer his question slide. "Don't we all." He finished the brew and set the empty cup beside him. "You know, I thought I found what I was looking for when I started the Seward office."

Davin paused. Was he really ready to speak the words out loud — that there might be more he wanted than making a name for himself as an FBI agent?

Paul chuckled. "She tends to do that to people."

"Do what?" Davin placed his elbows on his knees and turned his head to face Paul.

"Gets others to write their own story. She has this way of making you admit your deepest secrets and desires, even if you didn't know you had them to begin with." Paul slapped him on the shoulder. "I'm going to see if I can garner an update."

Davin's phone rang, stopping him from following Paul to the reception desk. Hollands.

"Sir. Any updates?"

"The complex has been cleared for occupancy and Senator Schulz plans to do the opening keynote speech in an hour."

The stubborn old man was going to get himself killed. Davin took a deep breath. "He does realize that the men who tried to kill him are still at large?"

SAC Hollands grunted. "The senator is well aware of the situation. He said that the secret service and FBI are highly trained operatives who know how to do their job."

Great. His own father would have no problem also blaming the two if something went wrong.

Davin needed to know the threat still out there. Nalani words haunted him. *I'm on that list too.*

"Any leads on Ian or Gregor?"

Hollands snapped his fingers and voices in the background responded to the nonverbal command. "They were last spotted heading towards the campus. We have agents with eyes on their camper, or what's left of it. I doubt they will return, but I'm not taking any chances."

"It makes sense that they'd head to the summit since it's still going to go on as if there wasn't any threat to human life." Davin let the sarcasm drip from each word.

"Look, Special Agent Schulz, I'm not going to pretend to understand your family dynamics, but I do know that I need one of my best agent's head in the game. Is that understood?"

The reprimand stung, but it was enough for him to snap out of his frustration. "Understood."

"You and VanKirk need to go through the summit program and identify any potential targets. Ian didn't succeed, but I'm sure he will try again."

"We will, sir."

Paul returned with a scowl on his face.

"One more thing, Schulz." Hollands' voice brooked no argument which meant he probably wasn't going to like the order. "Alexei wants regular updates on his daughter."

Dread churned his stomach. He of all people should not judge someone by the members of their family, but the desire to protect Nalani from anyone had him wanting to defy orders.

"We will keep everyone apprised of her progress," he gritted out.

He put his phone back in his pocket and looked at Paul's drawn face. Davin wanted to shake him so he'd spill the update.

"Ian gave her a high dose of Warfarin, which is preventing her blood from clotting." He ran his hand through his hair. "They are scanning her for any major internal bleeding, but they won't know if there was any brain damage until she wakes up."

Paul's words stole Davin's breath. Tears stung the backs of his eyes as he focused on his breathing. He couldn't lose her now. He had just found her.

He blew out a stuttered breath and prayed God would heal her.

"They are taking her upstairs as soon as she is back from radiology." Paul stood and started to pace back and forth.

Davin felt that same tension rising in him. He could go for a run or hit the gym, but he wouldn't leave the hospital until Nalani was leaving with him.

Davin stood in Paul's pacing pathway. "Hollands wants us to go over the summit's program and see if we could figure out a potential target for Ian."

Paul stared at him hard. He worked his jaw, but said nothing.

Davin folded his arms across his chest. "The best thing we can do for Nalani right now is find this guy so that she doesn't have to wake up still in the nightmare that Ian is roaming free."

Davin pulled up the program's schedule. "We know that Ian is after Alexei and the senator."

"If he could only go after one of them, it will be Alexei." Paul stared at Davin's phone screen. "Are there any presentations that were sponsored by Alexei's company? Or ones that would promise new technology that would lessen the environmental impact on Alaska?"

Davin looked at his friend waiting, for an explanation.

"Alexei is a business man at heart. If his company is supporting efforts, then he will be there to show his face. He won't pass on an opportunity to get in on ground breaking tech, either."

There was a breakout session tomorrow about policy being presented to the Alaskan government about mining practices that Alexei's company was given credit to help write.

"Look." Paul pointed to a different breakout session. "This is about new battery technology that would lessen the impact on the environment. This would be something that Alexei would be interested in."

"True, but there are other new sessions boasting about lessening the environmental impact." Davin looked at his fellow agent. "Why did this one stick out?"

Paul gave a slow grin. "Because this one mentions that it would move away from lithium, cobalt, and copper. Ian found copper on land his family owned many generations ago. Alexei knows this too."

Paul let the information hang in the air like a fog settling into the valley. Alexei would have a chance to, in his own way, stop or at least slow down his own son. Would he take it?

"I'm going to update Hollands." Davin pulled his phone back out. "I think I'll have a chat with Alexei. You find out what room they took her to."

Paul stalked back over to the nurse's station. Davin tapped his phone on his leg. It was time for him to have a conversation with the businessman. He just prayed he could trust the man to do the right thing.

Nalani could hear voices, but they were too far away to make out any words. She rolled her head to the side. Was that someone snoring? She willed her eyes to open, but they wouldn't budge. Why couldn't she open her eyes? The sounds slowly faded and she felt herself slip away. Again.

There was something warm on her hand this time. She tried to move it away, but whoever was there gripped her hand firmly.

"Nalani." The voice was rough, but it was the one that she had wanted to hear for days. She blinked open her eyes and this time they worked.

"Davin. You found me." The few words had her coughing and something slid across her cheek. Davin used his free hand to fix the plastic tubing.

"Keep that on until the doctor says it's okay to take it off."

The reality of the last few days washed through her as she winced. She was so focused on stopping the bomb that she forgot to ask about her brother. She swallowed. "Paul. Is he alive?"

As if saying his name could summon him, her brother walked through the door carrying two coffees. Butterfly bandages trailed across his forehead and his eyes were blackened, but he was still here. Still alive.

He handed a coffee to Davin and stood at the foot of the bed. "I thought I told you to call me when she woke up."

"She just regained consciousness." Davin took a sip of coffee, completely ignoring Paul's demanding tone. "I haven't even had a chance to call in the nurse or doctor."

Paul relaxed a bit. "I'll go get a nurse." He tugged on her foot. "Glad to see you awake." His gaze flicked to Davin's hand in hers. His lips pressed together as he left the room.

"I don't think he likes this." She squeezed his hand.

"But do you?" Davin's hoarse whisper spread warmth through her.

"Very much so." Her reply sent a slow smile across his face, transforming him into an attractive and not-so-grumpy man.

"Nalani, when you..." Davin's words died when a nurse came bustling into the room with Paul on her heels.

"Excuse me, sir, but I need to get in here to check her vitals."

Davin squeezed her hand before letting it go and walked to where Paul stood in the corner of the room. The nurse checked the IV machine, took her blood pressure, and monitored her oxygen levels. As she was wrapping up the equipment, she leaned close. "He hasn't left this room since you arrived yesterday."

Nalani followed the nurse's gaze to where Paul and Davin stood talking quietly. Davin's shoulders stiffened and a knot formed in her chest. What was going on?

"He looks like a grumpy grizzly, but around you he's more like a fluffy teddy." The nurse gave her a wink. "Hold on to that one."

Nalani's heart wanted to swell with all that the nurse's words implied, but the tension rolling off of Davin as he walked toward her put any dreams of happily ever after on hold for the moment.

"What's going on?" Nalani asked as soon as the door closed behind her nurse. "Don't tell me *nothing,* because he" —she lifted her chin towards Paul— "won't make eye contact with me and your shoulders are so tight I want to order you to go home and soak in a hot tub."

Davin gave her a half smile. "I'll only go if you go with me."

Paul made a gagging noise.

"Nice try, but you won't distract me. Now spill." Nalani tried crossing her arms, but the bruises on her wrist from the cuffs made her lay them back down where they were.

"Told you she'd know," Paul said. Davin shot him a scalding look then blew out a breath as he sat in the chair next to her bed.

"Hollands just called." Davin picked up her hand again. Something she would never tire of feeling. "They have been trying to find Ian at the summit."

"He hasn't found him yet?" Her outburst earned her another coughing fit. She took a few long draws of oxygen through the cannula. "Sorry. I just want that creep behind bars."

He encircled her hand in his. "No need to apologize. We all want this guy found and put in jail where he can't hurt anyone again."

She gave him a small nod then he continued. "Paul and I have been running through the summit program figuring out where Ian will strike. Hollands got a tip and wants me and Paul to come in. Once they confirm Ian's location, it will be all hands on deck to make sure he doesn't slip away again."

"I don't see how this is a bad thing." Her eyes roamed over his features. There was worry etched in the planes of his face.

Davin ran his thumb over her knuckles. "It's not, but there is no way I am leaving you here alone."

"Then I'll go with you." The dizziness was manageable. As long as she moved slowly.

Davin stared at her.

"What?" She said as she pulled the covers back.

"You need to stay here and rest." He put his hand on hers to keep her still. "I'll just tell Hollands that I will be staying with you."

She dipped her chin and narrowed her eyes at him. "You really think that Hollands will want his best agent side-lined to guard duty?"

"I'm going to pretend that doesn't hurt." Paul bemoaned in the corner.

Nalani rolled her eyes. She had almost forgotten that her big brother was here too.

"I want the best to protect you. When Ian took you," Davin paused. A shine gathered in his eyes. "I've never been so scared or angry in my life."

Davin gave Paul a sideways glance. Her brother pushed himself off the wall and slipped silently through the door before Davin continued. "You, Nalani Price, are one amaz-ing woman. I'm not sure where this" —he pointed between the two of them— "may go, but I would like to walk that journey with you."

Nalani wasn't sure how this man plowed through all of her defenses or how much she cared for him to actually want to go on this journey with him too. Deep down she knew that he wouldn't leave her. Even though she wasn't sure if they could make things work, for the first time she wanted to try.

"I would like that very much, but you have to go capture Ian." She pulled off the nasal cannula and swung her legs to the side. Punching the nurse's button she stood. The room swayed a bit so she grabbed hold of the bed railing.

*Slow movements,* she reminded herself.

Her wobble had Davin standing and wrapping his arm around her waist. She wouldn't think about how she smelled compared to the clean soap that emanated from him.

The nurse rushed back into the room with Paul only a step behind her. The petite nurse put her hands on her hips. "And just where do you think you are going?"

"Leaving. The man who did this to me is going to be arrested by this guy." She rested her head on Davin's chest and noticed how the motion gave her comfort and strength. "But he refuses to leave my side, so I'm going with him."

The nurse pursed her lips and stared at Davin. "And you encouraged this?"

"Absolutely not." Davin's voice wasn't harsh, but his tone was hard, begging her to defy it. "I told her that she needed to stay here and that I would stay with her."

"Ah." The nurse relaxed and turned her focus on Nalani, "You lost a lot of blood. We need to run another blood draw to check on your numbers. The doctor won't release you until your blood counts are all within normal range."

She started towards Nalani to help her back into bed, but Nalani needed both Paul and Davin there to capture Ian. She needed this monster to be taken down.

"No." She pulled away from Davin slightly to show them and herself that she could stand on her own. "Call the doctor. Order the blood test. I'm leaving with them. They need to be able to end this nightmare."

Davin's hand made small circles between her shoulder blades, sending warmth through her whole body. "Hollands will get him. I need to know you are safe and healing."

She turned to face him so he could see how hard she was going to dig in. "I'll be safe because I'll be with you. I need both of you to do this for me. I need to know that this is over. I can rest when Ian is behind bars."

A traitorous tear streaked down her cheek. Davin cupped her face and brushed it away with his thumb. "If it means that much to you, let's make a plan to keep you safe."

# Chapter 16

The last three hours passed in a blur. Her latest numbers showed all of her counts within normal range, although her platelet count was still lower than what the doctor was hoping for.

Nalani stood there waiting for Paul to get the car with Davin's arm around her, wearing clothes Ertz had apparently bought for her while she was out. When she looked at him, he wore that same grumpy, no nonsense look he had when they first met. His eyes constantly swept the parking lot. It made her smile. She knew now it was his FBI-Special-Agent-let's-get-things-done look and he was focused on getting the job done. Of protecting her.

Without looking at her, he said. "What's so funny?"

She stepped back, but threaded their fingers together. "Nothing is funny. I'm just enjoying your many expressions."

That scored her a quirk of his lips. What would it be like if he kissed her? Would his day-old stubble tickle? The facial hair made him look rugged. She wasn't sure which she liked better though, the clean shaven put-together agent or the rough-around-the-edges wilderness man.

"My face can't be that interesting." He gave her a sideways glance as the car pulled up to them.

"I was thinking about how your beard would tickle if you kissed me." There her mouth went again without first stopping at her brain's filter. She gently touched his face. "Trying to decide if you look better with or without it."

He leaned in, brushing his cheek against hers. The stubble prickled her skin, setting little fires across her face. "We'll have to test your theory later."

He opened the back door for her, then scooted in beside her instead of taking the front seat next to Paul. The move surprised her, but she wanted him close to her so she schooled her reaction. Resting her head on his shoulder, she let his presence infuse her with strength.

"How do you think Ian will try to kill Alexei and the senator again?" She raised her head remembering something Ian said to her back at the campground. "Ian told me that Senator Schulz isn't as innocent as he seems. Do you know what he meant by that?"

His frow burrowed deeper. "I try to keep my distance from my father." He wove his fingers in hers and relaxed his face a bit. "Not because I know of any wrongdoings, but because I wanted to make my own way without his influence. For so long our family did nothing but help him further his political career. When I decided to apply for the agency, I made it a point to keep myself from him so that I could forge my own journey."

He ran a hand through his hair. "Could he be into something within the shade of gray? I can't answer that. For the last five years I've only ever talked with my mother over the phone. Yesterday was the first time I had seen my father since I graduated from Quantico. I took the open position in Anchorage, then helped open the field office in Seward. I wanted to be as far away from DC and my father's influence as I possibly could get."

She felt like there was more to the story than having a powerful father. Most children would want their father's influence to help them, but she could see how that influence could lead to self-doubt. Having grown up without parents who could have made the way easier for her, she understood the drive to make something of your life on your own. The respect she had for him grew. He could have used the power his father clearly wielded to further himself. Instead, he fought for a path that he had to forge on his own.

"The thing is, no matter how hard I tried to outrun my father, he was still trying to control my life." He paused and she decided to wait him out. "Turned out the director of the FBI and my father are golfing buddies and he tried to get me placed near DC."

She drew her eyebrows together. "But you just said you went to Anchorage from Quantico?"

A small smile lifted his lips, "Apparently, Hollands went to bat for me after my interview. I have no idea what he said, but it worked. I owe him a debt of gratitude."

She rested her head back on his shoulder. Her energy was waning. Not like she'd fight any excuse to be close to Davin. "As do I."

Her eyes fluttered open at the sound of a door opening. She hadn't meant to fall asleep, but Davin made her feel comfortable, protected enough for her to fully relax.

The reality of where they were and who was there hit her full force, shoving the fatigue out of her mind. Ian was here somewhere and they needed to find him before he killed more people.

The campus was full of people milling about, unaware of the danger that walked among them. What would he do? Where was he?

The grounds looked like a typical college campus with academic buildings connected by walkways and roads surrounded by well manicured landscaping. It wasn't what she was expecting in the middle of Alaska, but she wasn't sure what she expected. Rough hewn structures peaking through pines? That was a bit juvenile, but this facility rivaled many college campuses she had been on over the years.

"This is impressive." She gave a low whistle.

Davin bit his lip, fighting the smile that wanted to take over his face. "Not what you expected?"

"Way better," she admitted.

"When we're not trying to catch a crazy man, I'll get you a tour of my alma mater. Who knows, there might be a story here somewhere."

She waved her hand in the direction of the huge sign that read, 'Alaska's Minerals: A National Strategic Imperative'. "There most certainly is. It might give me a reason to stay for a while."

Davin's eyes widened a bit and his lips parted. He searched her face before he spoke. "I would like that." He leaned in and kissed her on the temple. "Let's put Ian away for good and then we can talk more about you staying."

Her skin tingled where his day old growth touched, sending a smile along her lips. "We should find Hollands and get this over with quickly because I very much want to get to the staying part."

That earned her a small chuckle, a sound she hoped to hear often. He led her to a massive building with the words, 'College of Natural Science and Mathematics Murie Building' plastered on the side.

They made their way to the third floor at the end of the hall to a smaller classroom. Hollands had pushed together two tables and papers and laptops were spread across them. The front screen was displaying a schedule of the minerals summit along with a map of the campus.

Hollands' head lifted as they entered and the bear of a man strode towards them. His scowl matched his size, making Nalani grateful she was on his side. She could only imagine his sheer presence in the director's office being enough to persuade him to send Davin to Alaska. She swallowed back the jitters that ran through her body. If he threw her out of his command post, she wasn't sure even the president could stop him.

"I'm glad to see you up and walking again." His shoulders relaxed and his face softened ever so slightly. "You had two of my best agents on their knees begging God to bring you through."

Davin's hand tightened on hers and she took a glimpse over her shoulder at Paul. "The prayers worked. Now it's time to catch the man responsible for this mess."

Her spunk scored a half smirk from Hollands, which she was counting to as close to a full smile as the man would give. He didn't seem the type to fully let go until the mission was complete or even at all. He led them to the table, explaining where the sightings of Ian had occurred over the last day.

The cell phone on the table started to vibrate and Hollands snatched it up. "Hollands."

He worked his jaw while he listened. When he gripped the phone, causing his knuckles to turn white before he muted the phone and starting barking orders, Nalani knew this wasn't going to be an easy fight.

"Send me the recording. Thank you for your help." Hollands hung up and tossed his phone across the table. Placing his hands on his hips, he took a few deep breaths. Ian had no idea who he was going up against which gave her a bit of peace that this was going to end. And if SAC Hollands had anything to do with it, it would end soon.

Finally, he returned to the table, "We need to get agents to the second floor. Someone just reported to campus police that there was a man holding a room full of people hostage. They have the campus fire and EMTs on standby, but asked us to assess the situation since the man described matched Ian's picture we gave them."

Davin suited up with Paul, Ertz, and Burton. They would use the room next door to the classroom to try and get eyes on the situation. They needed to confirm there was a hostage situation, who was being held by whom, and where everything was located. It was imperative to know as many variables as possible in case they needed to breach. No one wanted someone to die because they weren't prepared.

Once they got their recon, Winters would open a line of communication and hopefully they'd be able to resolve this quickly. Being the smallest of the agents, Ertz volunteered to be the one to crawl up into the air duct. With feline finesse, she slid into the cramped dark space. Reaching down her hand, Paul gave her a snake camera adapted with a small motor to allow it to be moved by remote control.

From his vantage point at the door, Davin itched to get moving. How much longer would it take her to get the pictures they needed? His legs burned with the pent up energy. Finally, her head popped through the opening. "Ian has about twenty-five people huddled in the back of the room. Give me the pod, I think I can get us a live feed."

Planting a 360 camera would give them an advantage, but mounting it would cause some noise. "You'll need a distraction." Davin opened the door as Paul's warnings faded into the background.

He gave Ertz a few minutes to get into position. Praying for the right words and to not make the situation worse, Davin filled his lungs then called out. "Ian. We haven't officially met, I'm Special Agent Davin Schulz."

A low chuckle filter under the door. "The senator's boy. Tell me. Do you know what kind of business he deals in?"

He would not let Ian railroad him into some mind game. "I've been told that you are holding some innocent people hostage."

"I'll take that as a yes, and you approve of your father's dealings." Disgust dripped from Ian's voice.

Feet being shuffled backwards made his heart tick up a few notches. He needed to give Ertz more time. "Until yesterday, I hadn't seen or spoken to my father in five years. What he does is on his own shoulders, not mine." Not exactly where he wanted the conversation to go, but if it kept him talking then he'd do it.

"Sometimes fathers can be a disappointment." Ian's flat voice spoke louder than the words he uttered.

"Camera is live." Ertz's voice came through the coms. Davin took a step back towards his team.

"Stay in position," Hollands ordered. "Winters will coach you through this negotiation."

"You've already made a connection with him. Build on it." Mylee's calm helped lower his rattled brain. "Keep your voice low and smooth. You need to ask him what he wants."

He had attended one seminar on negotiations last year, but he was not a trained negotiator. With a quick prayer, he called out to Ian again. "We all make mistakes sometimes. What is it that you want, Ian?"

"I want...I want..." The door rattled as something crashed against it. Davin held his position when a tap on his arm broke his gaze from the door. Ertz handed him a small screen. Ian paced back and forth at the front of the room and a chair lay in front of the door.

"I want what is rightfully mine." One of the hostages shifted and Ian's gun flew in that direction. The woman's eyes widened and her body went rigid. Behind her now the camera could see clearly. There, sitting as if there wasn't a gun wielding mad man in the room, was Alexei Volkov sporting a bloodied lip. Next to him sat none other than Senator Schulz. Davin pushed the groan that wanted to escape back down. Why did they think it a wise thing to continue to be seen together after the bomb scare?

"You need to keep him talking. If we can figure out what he wants, we have a bargaining chip." Winters coached through the earpiece.

"What is that, Ian?" Davin shouted towards the door while keeping his eyes on the screen.

Ian barked. "I thought you were better than that, Agent Schulz. Did you get your agent back in one piece?"

"I will let him know about your concern for his well being." Davin watched Ian return to pacing at the front of the room. "There are innocent people in there with you.

How about we make a trade? You let  everyone go and I will get you one thing you need right now."

Ian's jaw clenched then a slow smirk ticked up the sides of his mouth. "I'll give you the innocents, if you give me Nalani. I plan to take over the family business and I would rather not share."

Anger boiled hot within him and the 'no' raced to rip out of his mouth, but Winters was in his ear, "Tell him you will work on his request. Then report back here where we can make a plan."

"I'm going to have to talk with the Special Agent in Charge."

"You have ten minutes then the first person dies."

Davin raced back to the command center, where he found Paul with his arm around Nalani, who looked paler and so very small. There was no way they were sending her back into arm's reach of that psycho. The clicking of the shutting door had Nalani's eyes snapping to his. She tore away from Paul and engulfed him in a vise around his waist.

"What were you thinking?" She shoved him backwards. "Ian has no soul. He could have easily shot you dead." Her eyes reddened and unshed tears glistened in the room's overhead light. Davin could feel the stares of the other agents in the room.

"God was with me and I needed to give Ertz an opportunity to plant the camera. Now we can see everything that Ian is doing." He rubbed her arms as she dashed away a runaway tear.

"Ian wants to kill me." Her small shattered voice withdrew his last resolve as he pulled her toward himself. He tucked her under his chin and just held on. This strong brilliant woman was terrified and he wouldn't let Ian anywhere near her.

He looked towards Hollands. "Please tell me you have a plan."

"How are your acting skills?" Hollands crossed his arms across his chest and spread his feet apart while looking him up and down.

If it meant keeping Nalani safe and stopping Ian, he'd give the performance of a lifetime. Davin nodded and Hollands launched into his plan. With everyone's jobs distributed, each agent double checked their gear and headed to their post.

Nalani tugged on his arm to stop him from leaving with the others. "Please be careful." She stepped up on her tiptoes and gave him a soft kiss. One that spoke of desires for the future, sweetness, and trust.

"Mmm. Just as wonderful as I thought."

Her dark eyes opened, pulling him back towards her lips. This time he held little back, cupping the back of her head to pull her closer. She ran her fingers on his beard and around his neck like he was the one holding her up. He didn't care how she destroyed his well laid walls, all that mattered was that she was here.

Someone clearing their throat made him pull back, but he kept his hand on her back. "To be continued?"

She grinned. "Go get him Mr. Special Agent."

Davin turned to see Paul glaring at him, but the twitch of his lips gave away his failing attempt to hide his smile. "We can do without that again," he deadpanned, then looked past Davin and winked at Nalani, "But as long as my baby sis is happy, I'm happy."

Davin leaned in and kissed her cheek. "Pray for me," he whispered into her ear. His hand ran down her arm pulling it gently with him as he walked slowly towards the door.

"Always." She squeezed his hand and let him go. Now he only had to trick a psychopath into turning himself in. What could possibly go wrong?

# Chapter 17

D avin stood by the door to the classroom again, this time with every intention of getting himself inside. Winters stood beside him with the small screen in her hand. She would stay in this position, continuing to coach him as long as Ian didn't find his ear wig.

She gave him a nod then he called out. "Ian. I've got some bad news."

A scream was muted by the door but Davin saw Ian grab a woman and shove his gun against her head via the camera. "Nalani better be there or this woman dies."

Davin swallowed. Here went nothing. "Nalani is in a coma. She can't be here even if she wanted to help us."

"Then I guess we are at an impasse." Ian tipped the woman's head back. "And what a shame to waste such beauty."

"Wait." Davin watched as Ian paused in pressing the weapon further into her neck. "I know I'm not Nalani, but I am a federal agent. Release all of the innocent people in the room and take me in their stead. We can try to work out a deal after they are all released."

"How noble of you." Ian chuckled. "Must get that from your mother."

Ian didn't say anything else or release the woman. Davin prayed harder. *God, help us.* As the words lifted from him, Ian shoved the woman toward the desk at the front of the room.

He grabbed Alexei, Harrison, and another man, throwing each of them towards where the woman now stood. Waving his gun at the rest of the small group, he demanded, "The rest of you line up by the door. Agent Schulz, you have thirty seconds to remove them from the room and appear in their spot before I start killing them."

Davin threw open the door and the people started running. Paul led them away to be debriefed and treated for any injuries.

When Davin stepped into the room, he held his hands high.

"Throw your weapon out the door and close it behind you." Spit flew from Ian's mouth.

Davin took his holstered Sig Sauer and skidded it across the floor, then closed the door. He took in the room and the four remaining people. "I thought we had a deal. Myself for all of the innocent people in the room. I know you have issues with our fathers, but those two..."

"Stop talking now or I'll silence you." Davin closed his mouth.

"Don't push him right now. Give him the appearance of power and control, because that's what he needs in this moment," Winters coached. Davin wanted to disarm him and take him in, but from this distance he wouldn't be able to make it two steps before Ian shot him.

"Ian, you are bringing shame to the Volkov name." Alexei spoke low.

Ian swung his gun towards his father. "You are the one who abandoned your family." A vein bulged in his neck. "*You* are a disappointment to our fathers who ruled with fear and respect."

"There is no respect in being a criminal," Alexei said coolly.

Ian took another step towards the small group. Alexei stepped to the front as if he was protecting the others behind him. Davin took advantage of the distraction and moved closer. If he could get close enough, the agents on the other side of the door could be in here in a second. He just hoped they knew what he was planning. It wasn't the original game plan, but when the opportunity to end this appeared, he knew he had to take it. Only a few more steps.

"I did not abandon you. I sent you to the very best schools, taught you the value of hard work." Alexei took another small step closer and Davin matched his step. He wasn't sure what the man had in mind. He only needed him to keep Ian distracted. Not take Ian out by himself.

"You call sending me away to an international school and then university in America for business not abandoning me? You couldn't stand the greatness you saw in me so you cast me aside in hopes that it would die." Ian beat his chest with his free hand. "Grandfather was the only one who wanted me to flourish."

"Ian," Alexei boomed, making Ian's nostrils flare as puffs of breath heaved his chest. He switched to Russian. Davin's language skills were rusty, but he was able to make out most of what Alexei said. "Grandfather is not well. He believes that the Cold War is still a thing and that the motherland should take back everything that was once theirs."

Davin tucked that information away for when they got themselves out of here and were tying up this case. Only one more step to go. Ian's ire was rising, but his grip on his gun still held steady.

"Stop this now and I'll call in a few favors." Alexei switched back to English.

"I don't need your favors." Ian swung at that moment towards Davin who dove as the crack of the gun broke the air. Fire tore through the outside of his shoulder, but he gripped the gun as he rolled to the side.

Alexei tackled Ian.

Davin raced towards the others shouting as he ran. "Get down." He pushed them behind the desk at the front of the room and stood in a tucked stance between them and the two Volkovs.

The door flew open and agents streamed into the room. "FBI! Everybody down!" Ian had flipped his father over holding him in a choke hold as agents surrounded them on two sides.

"Release him." Hollands commanded. He was standing to the right of the two in the middle of the room with no one behind them from that standpoint. If anyone was going to have to neutralize the suspect, Hollands was the only one with a clear shot.

Ian stared at Hollands for a moment then he shifted his arms. The movement allowed Alexei to thrust his arms up to break out of Ian's hold and throw him to the ground. Four agents descended on the two. Alexei stepped away once Hollands had secured Ian and started reading him his Miranda Rights.

Ian chose not to invoke his right to remain silent as he yelled, "You will all pay for this. Spartak will live on."

Two agents drug him out the door as he arched his back, fighting the restraints. His face was red and rage vibrated off of him. "Nothing will stand in the way of the motherland."

His shouts in Russian faded with the closing of the door.

Davin turned towards the three behind him and helped them to their feet. Harrison Schulz slapped him on his shoulder. "Thanks, son. You are a great agent. I'm proud of you."

He stopped seeking his father's approval long ago, but the words still found a way to parts of his heart that he had shut down. "I'm just thankful no one else was injured."

Davin turned to Alexei. "Thank you for the distraction."

"One never wants to believe the evil that their family is capable of until they can no longer deny it." Alexei frowned and stared at the door. He ran a hand through his hair, mussing the perfect style.

Davin put a hand on the man's shoulder. "We cannot change who our family is, nor are we responsible for the choices they made."

Alexei nodded and sighed. "True."

"I'm not sure I would waste any favors for him." This from Harrison.

Alexei stood a bit taller. "He is still my son even though he deserves to go to jail for a long time. I need to call my lawyer. He'll need someone to walk him through pleading guilty."

The door burst open and Nalani flew into the room. Alexei took in a sharp breath.

"Sorry, sir. I couldn't stop her." Ertz glared at Nalani, who continued to stare at Alexei.

Alexei took a step towards her. "Lorelai." The name barely a whisper.

Tears formed in Nalani's eyes as she shook her head. Her father stood in front of her with so much hope and love glimmering behind his wide eyes. In so many ways he looked like Ian, but there was a light in him that was absent in his son. He wasn't a soulless monster that she needed to fear.

She found her voice finally. "My name is Nalani. I believe I am your daughter."

He wrapped her in solid arms and she let the levy on her emotions break. Her shoulders heaved up and down with bone rattling sobs. For how many years did she long for someone to hold her like this? To have someone who was her own blood want her?

He pulled back, cupping her face with his hands and swiping away the tears with his thumbs. "When I found out Lorelai had a child, I looked for you. I hired the best PI I could find to track you down."

He had looked for her? Then the sensation she felt before she left of someone following her was real and it was him. Well, the person he hired to find her.

He tucked her hair behind her ear and just stared at her face. "He told me that he had a lead, but you had disappeared. You look so much like her." His chin began to quiver and she felt the rise of a second wave of tears. Enclosing her in another strangling hug, he kissed her head then let her go.

"Come, we have much to talk about. I want to learn all about the adventures you have had." His smile melted the last of the ice away. She had a family and they wanted her.

Someone beside her cleared his throat. "I'm sorry to stop this family reunion, but we need to take everyone's statements and finish collecting evidence." Davin stood only a few feet away from her. Not touching her physically, but his presence was giving her strength. She had gone from a lonely woman standing on her own to having two men who wanted to be there to support her. The thought had her heart swelling with joy.

"Let's get this done." Nalani reached out for Davin's hand, which he gladly surrendered to her.

Three hours with a sketch artist and another hour with two different agents, Nalani was done giving her statement and retelling the sordid story over and over again. She wasn't sure if she made it clear that Gregor, or whatever his real name was, was actually a good guy, or at least mostly a good guy. He did help Ian escape to the college and he drove the camper van to Fairbanks, but he was the only reason that Davin and Paul found her before she and the bomb made it to campus. That had to count for something. Right? She would let the FBI sort that whole mess out and said a prayer for Gregor. He seemed trapped and she wanted to rewrite his story to set him free.

Davin leaned against the wall opposite the door of the conference room. He removed himself from the interviews because of his "attachment" to the victim. The phrase he used before he gave her a peck on the temple and sent her into the room an hour ago. She very much loved the sound of that and the feel of his lips on her skin. He had shaven and showered while she was in the interview. The smell of soap wafted to her as he stood to greet her.

"You did great."

She laid her head on his solid chest letting him hold her in the cocoon that was beginning to feel like home. Like safety. Like love. She sighed.

"You weren't there. I could have made a fool of myself," she mumbled into his shirt.

She felt the vibrations from his chuckle on her cheek, "I find it hard to believe that the fearless Nalani Price could make a fool of herself." He tipped her chin towards him and covered her lips with his own. The kiss was soft, but filled with promises of a future. She ran her hand along his smooth jaw and dove her fingers into his hair. Her heart burst with the hope of a future filled with someone who cared, who wouldn't leave her. A soft moan escaped her, which made him pull her closer. Yes, this was her safe place. No matter what life threw at her, here in Davin's arms she could find love and acceptance.

She trailed kisses down his jaw until she was able to whisper in his ear, "Thanks for staying."

"Mmm." His low timber sent gooseflesh down her arms, "I will always be here for you."

She didn't care what it took, she would find a way to stay. To take a chance on them.

"Well, I hope this makes my offer a bit easier to persuade you to take." Nalani jumped back from Davin, but he snaked his arm around her waist and pulled her to his side. Tucked in like it was where she always belonged.

"What offer would that be?" Nalani asked as she faced Alexei who stood there with a knowing look on his face.

"I want you to come work for my company. We help businesses come up with action plans and proposals. In particular, when it has to do with the environmental impact that company will have." Surprise rippled through her. "Not what you were expecting?"

A light blush warmed her cheeks. "Not exactly. Your reputation isn't the tree hugger type."

Alexei threw his head back and laughed. It was nothing like the laughter that came from Ian. No, this sounded more like love and merriment. Nalani couldn't help the grin that tugged at her own lips.

Alexei sobered, "When your mother died, I made myself a fortress in the business world, but the joy I had with her never came back. No matter how many deals I closed." He gave her a sad smile. "One day, Ian asked me why I kept a picture of Lorelai on my desk. The memories of her flew through my mind and made me take a hard look at myself. She wouldn't have been pleased with who I had become, so I changed my company's mission. She was always conscious of how we were affecting the earth and how we needed to protect it not for us, but for our children and grandchildren. Now I help other companies protect nature as a way to honor her. And you."

The weight of not being able to ever meet her mother laid heavy on her shoulders, but she would do what she could to make her mother proud. "I don't know much about environmental laws or how to make a business deal, but I would like to honor her too."

"Stop by my office in Anchorage tomorrow morning and I'll have a contract for you to sign. I could use an editor on my staff to make sure there are no mistakes in the deals we draw up. I can teach you the rest of the business as we go."

Editing was something that she could do. With her contacts in the journalism world, she could still do a bit of freelance writing. The possibilities were forming in her mind. For the first time in her life, she didn't feel the need to wander from place to place chasing a story because she had found her home. She was sure that she and Davin would still travel, but now she had a base to call hers. A place to belong.

"That sounds great." She faced Davin. "Do you mind if we stay one more night?"

"If it means you're staying in Alaska, I'll do whatever it takes."

"One more thing." Alexei looked straight at her. "Just let your papochka know when the wedding will be."

She wasn't sure about what Davin thought of a wedding, but her heart longed for that day.

Alexei then sent a stern look towards Davin. "I only just found her, keep her safe, son."

"I plan to for the rest of my life, if she'll let me."

# Acknowledgments

First and foremost, I thank God for the strength, inspiration, and guidance throughout this journey.

A heartfelt thank you to Lisa Phillips and Kate Angelo for believing in me from the very beginning. Your support and encouragement, as well as your invaluable brainstorming sessions, helped shape this story into something I am truly proud of. Lisa, your feedback and suggestions were instrumental in making the narrative stronger and more engaging, and for that, I am deeply grateful.

To Madisyn at Mountain Peak Editor, thank you for your meticulous editing and your dedication to making this book shine. Your skill and expertise have been vital in bringing my vision to life.

Seward, Alaska, your rugged beauty and rich history were the inspiration for the world I created within these pages. Thank you for being a place of inspiration, and for reminding me of the untamed spirit of the land and its people.

A special thank you to Two Dogs Publishing for giving me the incredible opportunity to publish my work and make this dream a reality.

Lastly, to my husband and sons—thank you for your unwavering support and encouragement. You believed in me, even on the days when I didn't believe in myself. Your patience as I poured myself into writing this story means more than words can express.

# About the author

**L**ily J. Hann writes Christian romantic suspense novels that intertwine thrilling mysteries with messages of faith and love. A devoted wife and mom, she cherishes time spent exploring life's adventures with her husband and two sons. When she's not writing or adventuring, you'll likely find her curled up with a good book or enjoying a quiet moment with a cup of coffee. Lily lives in Maryland, where her family and faith inspire her stories.

Be sure to subscribe to her newsletter for all of the latest on upcoming books.

*Scan and subscribe*
*to Lily's newsletter*

# Also by Lily Hann

**<u>New Freedom Fire and Rescue</u>**
Spotting the Fire
Flare Up (coming 2026)
**<u>Seward Field Office</u>**
Alaskan Family Ties
Alaskan Hero's Return (coming May 2026)

Visit www.lilyhannauthor.com for complete list of books
and ways to purchase all of your favorites.

# Sneak Peak at Alaskan Hero's Return

**S**ome lies cut deeper than betrayal. Some loves never die.

FBI agent and cyber expert Taylor Ertz has sworn off love. Three years ago, her fiancé vanished during a covert mission, presumed dead—but Taylor's heart refuses to believe it. Every search for answers has ended in silence and stone walls. Now, she's thrust undercover in Senator Schulz's PR team, posing as a web designer to unmask a mole feeding secrets to the Russians.

Kambre "Kam" King should have died three years ago. Once a loyal operative, he's been living as a ghost after his convoy was ambushed while transporting a Russian defector. The CIA declared him dead, along with the rest of his team. Now, as Spartak's deadly network resurfaces, Kam is sent in to sniff out the traitor among them in order to take down Spartak for good.

The CIA is convinced Taylor is the mole. Kam knows better—and he'll risk everything to clear her name, and earn back his freedom. But as old wounds collide with new danger, trust becomes their most powerful weapon—and their greatest vulnerability.

# Chapter 1

Kam King undid the top button of his dress shirt. He had ditched the tie. The tightened collar rubbed his scars. He didn't need a constant reminder of the prison in which he found himself. He adjusted the wig one last time and leaned toward the mirror to make sure the contacts changing his eye color were in place.

Tonight, he was Ryan McNite. Another name. Another mission. This life was wearing on him. He needed out.

Straightening he gave himself one last look over. It wasn't Hollywood-level disguise, but his job today was to keep to the shadows and observe. Someone on the Senator's payroll was conversing with Lysander. His handler told him to leave it alone, but if he could find a way to connect Lysander to a crime on US soil, he could finally shut down Spartak for good and leave this life behind him.

Taylor, sitting on the back porch swing at her parents' house sobbing, flashed in his mind. He closed his eyes and let the pain wash over him. She was never far from his thoughts. One day, he would take down Spartak and be able to return to his life. To her.

He shook his head. Who was he kidding? She probably didn't want anything to do with who he had become. He huffed. First, he would get out of the mess he woke up in then he could worry about what happened next.

He took a deep breath and stepped onto the elevator. "Here goes nothing."

The elevator music hummed softly, but did nothing to soothe the buzz in his veins. He leaned into the adrenaline, allowing it to sharpen his senses. The elevator dinged.

It was time to sniff out a traitor.

The chatter of voices and strum of classical music filtered their way to him from behind the large banquet hall doors. McNite was a wealthy businessman who donated to the Senator's campaign, or so his dossier read. Kam put on his brightest smile as he reached for the door handle.

The door launched at him, and he jumped back as a tall man in a black suit barreled into him. He had to use all of his restraint to not put the guy on the ground. The man turned toward him, and then he had to check his reaction again so that the recognition didn't show on his face. Paul VanKirk. What was the FBI agent doing in Seattle?

"Sorry about that, Sir," Paul said as he took a step away from Kam.

"Not a problem. Hope she's alright." Kam winked.

Paul stared at him.

"You were running out of there fast. I know only two things that could make a man run that fast. An emergency or a woman. Since there's no screaming, I assumed you're either chasing after or running from a woman." Kam smiled. Why was he engaging VanKirk? He should be making his way into the shadows. He was supposed to find a traitor, not try to make friends with the FBI agent he had beaten. He had done his best to pull his punches, but he had to make it believable. It was better than what Ian had planned for the agent.

Paul grumbled something about people with money while he turned from him. If Paul was here, Taylor could be here too. He had avoided confronting her last month when the Seward Field Office team took down Ian Volkov. Seeing her even from a distance made his desire to fight for his freedom burn brighter. She had no longer been a part of his dreams and memories, but there in the flesh. He couldn't put her at risk until he got himself out of this world though. He would get Lysander, then he would be done. He more than paid his debt to his country. It was time for him to retire and find out if Taylor could love the broken man he was now.

The room was warm as people sat and ate their dinners. Kam's phone dinged.

> You're at table 14.

Kam smirked. He knew that his handler couldn't resist the opportunity to take down Lysander. He wove his way through the tightly packed tables, looking for something. He wasn't sure what exactly, but he would know when he saw it.

Table 14 was on the edge of the room, partially in the shadows. Perfect. He could see and not necessarily be seen.

The string quartet packed up for the night as a DJ started to play an upbeat song. Looks like he missed the meal. It's just as well. He'd eat when he got back to his hotel. Now, he needed to focus on the room.

His gaze stopped at the edge of the dance floor. The woman looked like she'd be anywhere but talking with that guy but that wasn't what made his eyes stop their searching. The woman had short blonde hair, but he knew that face. It was still the face he saw in his dreams. The only one that kept him from going too deep into the darkness.

Taylor.

If that guy didn't take the hint that she was giving, Kam would have to break every rule tonight and go to her. His phone pinged with another message. Kam tore his eyes away from Taylor long enough to see that his handler sent him a picture.

**This is the target.**

This couldn't be right.

Are you sure the intel is solid?

**As solid as it can be.**

He stared at the picture. The hair matched the woman across the room, but those eyes-those were the same ones he fell in love with. There was no way that Taylor was the one contacting Lysander.

I'm going to make contact.

He could feel his phone vibrating as he slid it into his pocket. He was sure that his handler was waving him off. Reminding him that Lysander was the one they wanted, not the mole.

The man was still talking with Taylor. When he leaned into her space, Kam felt himself closing the gap faster than was probably necessary. The man reached up to touch her face, but Taylor grabbed his wrist and brought his arm down before pushing him away. Kam was close enough to hear them now.

"I said I wasn't interested in dancing. Now, if you don't mind, I need to use the ladies' room." Taylor spun right into Kam's path.

He taught her arms to straighten her. "I'm so sorry. I-" Kam cleared his throat and turned on his billionaire charm and fake accent. "Well, I was coming over to rescue you from a man who forgot how to be a gentleman, but I see my services are not needed."

Taylor stared at him, blinking slowly. How he missed those eyes. They were somehow more beautiful than he remembered. The way the dark brown melted into a golden ring around the outside mesmerized him.

She shook her head and took a step out of his reach. "You are quite right. I don't need you." She looked over Kam's shoulder, then back to him. "I'm sorry I didn't catch your name."

"Ryan McNite." The lie rolled off his tongue, but this time it tasted bitter. How he longed to just be Kam King. To go back to being in love with Taylor Ertz. To have a family and three little ones of their own.

Taylor stared at him a moment longer. "I'm Tina Miller." They were both pretending to be someone different tonight. She extended her hand. Instead of shaking it, he lifted it to his lips and kissed her knuckles. Electricity crackled through him at the feel of her hand pressed against his lips. The small gasp from her told him she felt something too.

"I have to go." She spun on her heels.

"I'm not great at dancing, but I like long walks on the beach." The first words he had spoken to her all those years ago had the desired effect because she stopped mid-stride and faced him. She tilted her head, looking him over. A shine came over her eyes, and she blinked it away.

"I prefer to sit and read a book." She took another step away from him. "I do have to go."

She called over her shoulder as she walked away, "Don't die before I get back. I have so many questions for you."

He watched her weave through the crowd and slip through the side door. His phone was vibrating in his pocket. He pulled it out to see who was calling him. Silencing the phone, he shoved it back into his pocket. His handler could wait. He needed to figure out who was framing Taylor. He broke so many rules tonight, but he didn't care. No one was going to get away with letting Taylor take the fall for their deeds. He'd do anything to get a second chance at his life again.